A SEAL's Courage

ALSO BY JM STEWART

The Seattle Bachelors Series
Bidding on the Billionaire
Winning the Billionaire
Bargaining for the Billionaire
Claiming the Billionaire

A SEAL's Courage

JM STEWART

New York Boston

Copyright © 2017 by JM Stewart
Excerpt from *A SEAL's Honor* copyright © 2017 by JM Stewart
Cover design by Brian Lemus
Cover copyright © 2017 by Hachette Book Group, Inc.

Forever Yours
Hachette Book Group
1290 Avenue of the Americas
New York, NY 10104
forever-romance.com
twitter.com/foreverromance

First ebook and print on demand edition: July 2017

Forever Yours is an imprint of Grand Central Publishing. The Forever Yours name and logo are trademarks of Hachette Book Group, Inc.

The publisher is not responsible for websites (or their content) that are not owned by the publisher.

The Hachette Speakers Bureau provides a wide range of authors for speaking events. To find out more, go to www.hachettespeakersbureau.com or call (866) 376-6591.

ISBN 978-1-5387-2884-0 (print on demand edition)
ISBN 978-1-5387-1173-6 (ebook edition)

This one is for all the men and women in the U.S. military. Thank you for your service and the sacrifices you make every day so that our world stays safe.

A SEAL's Courage

CHAPTER ONE

"I'm going to be a virgin until I die." Lauren Hayes let out a world-weary sigh and sank back against the plush leather seats. The club around her pulsed, the throbbing beat and surging bodies lending an upbeat atmosphere Lauren couldn't get into.

Stephanie Mason, one of her two best friends, peered over the rim of her drink, her straw dangling from the side of her mouth. "You need to give up your perfect-man wish list, babe, and settle for Mr. Right Now, because Mr. Right doesn't exist."

Lauren eyed the two women seated across the table from her and sighed. "I know it's old-fashioned, but I wanted my first time to be with someone who'd actually remember my name in the morning. Not some hookup in a bar."

Mandy Lawson, best friend number two, shook her head, sending her short dark curls swishing over her shoulder. "I'm afraid, sweets, as the saying goes, if you want to find Prince Charming, you have to kiss a few toads. You're not going to lose your virginity by being picky."

Mandy had been her best friend since junior high. They'd met in home ec when their teacher partnered them together for a project. She'd told Lauren long ago she was nuts for making that chastity pact in ninth grade. She and a few of the other girls from church promised to remain virgins until they married. At the time, Lauren had made it with good intentions. When she was ten, her birth mother died in a car accident while driving home from another date with yet another fling. Having a single mother who slept around so much she didn't even know who Lauren's father was had left a lasting impression. She'd grown up determined to never, *ever*, become like her mother.

Lauren waved a hand at Mandy. "Oh, I know, but it's hard to reconcile my ideas of how true love should be with the desire to lose my virginity as quickly as possible."

Lauren had strict rules for how she lived her life, things she'd gleaned from her adoptive mother, Mary. Mary had started out her foster mother, eventually adopting her when she was eleven. She'd gotten lucky. Not all kids who ended up in foster care got adopted. Mary had been a deeply religious woman and had old-fashioned ideas, particularly when it came to things like dating and sex. Never make the first move. No kissing on the first date. No drinking or staying out late. Number one on that list? No sex before marriage.

The problem was, Lauren had yet to do much actual living. She had yet to know the gloriousness of sex. Or getting so drunk she woke up the next day not remembering how she'd gotten home. Or hell, the simple pleasure of making out with a guy. Wasn't most of that normal teenage behavior?

Mary had lived a safe—but boring—life. Her strict rules had kept her from living as much as she could have. She'd devoted herself to the church and to raising Lauren, and had died in her sleep, in her favorite recliner with her knitting in her lap. Mary's death had hit Lauren hard. And it had taught her one thing: life was short. She wanted to have a little fun before she died. To give up "the rules" and do all those things she'd held back on out of fear of doing the wrong thing. So far she hadn't done any of that.

She picked up her drink—some fruity concoction with sex in the name, courtesy of Steph—and took a sip before eyeing the girls again. "It's sad, isn't it? I'll be twenty-eight next week, and I've never even fallen in love. Infatuation, sure, and something that felt an awful lot like love until I realized it was one-sided."

Across the table, Stephanie waggled her blond brows. "Just do it, babe. Go dance, rub up against some hottie, and let nature takes its course."

Oh, she'd tried that. After Mary's death, she'd jumped into the dating pool, determined to get herself out there. She'd signed up for several of those dating sites and had gone on plenty of dates. The problem was, they never went anywhere. More than a few of the men wanted nothing to do with a virgin. Some had been a little *too* eager for her tastes. Most, though, had simply never called her back before she'd even gotten around to admitting that she was a virgin.

Lauren shook her head. "I agree it's time, but that's not me. Hell, I'd probably trip over my own feet and make a complete dork of myself."

She was born with the klutz gene. If she didn't watch the ground when she walked, she tended to trip over stuff. She couldn't count the number of times she'd run into a pole or another person because she'd been too wrapped up in her thoughts.

"You know…" Mandy, who was a little more down to earth, took a moment to gulp down the last of her beer. She set the bottle on the table and leaned forward to grin at Lauren. "I could always—"

"Oh, no." Lauren laughed and held up her hands. She didn't need to ask to know where this was going. Mandy loved playing matchmaker. "No way am I letting you fix me up again. You're a fabulous wedding designer, sweetie, but your taste in men sucks. There was Jake the octopus, who had eight arms and wouldn't take no for an answer. And then there was Guy, who talked about himself all night and how wonderful he was. Need I go on?"

Mandy's bottom lip popped out, but her cheeks flushed bright crimson. "Aw, come on. They weren't all awful. I know a hot military guy who'd be right up your alley…"

Lauren laughed again and jabbed a pointed finger at Mandy. "No."

"Actually…" Mandy looked to her left, flagging down the waitress and signaling for a refill by holding up her empty beer bottle. When the waitress smiled and nodded, Mandy turned back around and leaned her elbows on the table. "There's a new dating service I just heard of. You remember Jennifer Dillon, from high school?"

Lauren nodded. "Didn't I see an engagement announcement in the paper last week?"

"Yup. She and her fiancé came into my office the other day for help planning the wedding. In fact, I recommended your bakery for the cake. Ohhh, Laur, you should have seen her fiancé. He's air force. Tall, broad shouldered, and so polite. Came in dressed in his uniform, all 'yes, ma'am' and 'no, ma'am.'"

Lauren sipped at her drink. "No. I'm not letting you set me up again. I don't care if he's got a brother or friends or a million bucks."

Mandy furrowed her brow, glaring in disapproval. "Will you just listen? While we were talking about her wishes for the ceremony, I asked her where she'd met him. She said they used this service. Military Match. Kind of pricey, but the woman who runs it screens her applicants. So when I went home that night, I checked it out online." Mandy's blue eyes gleamed with impishness. "All the men are vets."

"Oh, I'm definitely in." Steph nudged Lauren with an elbow. "So are you."

Lauren couldn't stop the fierce heat that flooded her cheeks. These ladies knew her too well. Okay, she had to admit it. She had a "thing" for military men. There was something about a guy who willingly put his life on the line for people who couldn't fight for themselves. The uniform alone could melt her panties.

She sipped at her icy drink in a vain attempt to cool down. "I don't know what you're talking about."

Mandy laughed. "Right. Don't think I never noticed the way you'd go all tongue-tied whenever Trent came home on leave."

Steph turned her head, winking at Lauren. "Or the way you drool when he walks away from you."

Mandy was the youngest of three. Her brothers were ten years older than her and twins. Trent and Will might look identical, but the two couldn't be more different. Will was clean-cut. The guy in suits and ties rather than jeans and worn T-shirts. Trent had always been rough around the edges, a quiet guy who preferred to work with his hands.

A Navy SEAL, he'd gotten out of the service and returned home eighteen months ago with scars, some visible, some not. He now worked in a custom motorcycle shop doing detail work. Of the two brothers, Trent was the one who had always made her cream her panties. More to the point, Mandy knew she had a crush on him.

Steph looked over at Mandy. "How he's doing anyway?"

Mandy shook her head and sighed. "He's...different. He's always been quiet, but he crawled into himself after he came home and hasn't come back out yet."

Trent had post-traumatic stress disorder. Nightmares. Flashbacks. Coming home, he'd had a hell of a time of it. Mandy was right. He was doing better these days, but he still wasn't the guy he'd been before his last deployment.

Lauren dropped her gaze, pretending to be absorbed in her drink. "You should sign *him* up for that dating service. Might do him some good."

Mandy laughed. "Nope. He won't let me fix him up, either." Mandy rose to her feet and came around the table, tugging Lauren out of her seat. "Come on, ladies. Let's go find us some hotties and shake our tail feathers."

* * *

The following evening, Lauren pulled open her front door to find Mandy standing on her doorstep. She wore a sheepish grin Lauren had seen too many times over the years. It usually meant trouble.

Lauren folded her arms, narrowing her gaze. "All right. What did you do?"

Mandy's cheeks blazed bright red, and she took sudden interest in her sneakers. "I signed you up. I signed us all up, actually."

Lauren's heart took off on a one-hundred-meter dash. She had a sneaking suspicion she knew what Mandy referenced, but she needed to hear her headstrong best friend own up to it. "Signed us up for what?"

"That dating agency." Mandy looked up then, flashed a *please-don't-be-mad* grin, and clasped her hands together. "Steph's excited about it…"

Lauren's eyes widened. "Oh my God, Mandy. How could you do that? You don't know anything about this woman or this service."

"Actually, I do." Mandy stepped over the threshold, grabbed Lauren's wrist, and after closing the front door, pulled her into the living room. Once there, she took a seat on the sofa and patted the spot beside her. "I know I can be a little…impulsive, but I went to talk to the woman. She won't let me sign you up officially until you come down to speak to her yourself. Laur, you'd like her. Turns out, Karen's husband works with Trent at the bike shop. She's really down to earth and sweet. She's a great big romantic, but she's strong minded, like you. She wants her clients to feel comfortable with their experience, whether it lasts or not."

Lauren dropped onto the sofa beside her. Okay, so she was impressed Mandy hadn't rushed headlong into this, but she had enough experience with Mandy not to let her off the hook yet. "You should've consulted me first."

Mandy nudged her with an elbow. "Come on. You know you would've said no. Besides." Mandy dropped back against the sofa cushions with a tired sigh. "Jennifer was so happy when she came into my office the other day. I mean glowing. So is Skylar. The expression on her face when she looks at Will? I've never seen him so calm or so happy. I want that. One guy who makes me feel feminine and beautiful, who isn't turned off by the fact that I can take care of myself. Clearly I won't find it on my own."

Lauren leaned back and lay her head against Mandy's. "Me, either."

Mandy reached for her hand. "So do this with me. Us. Go talk to Karen and decide for yourself. You're right, you know. You shouldn't lose your virginity to some jerk you meet in a bar. Or in the back of a Toyota like I did."

Lauren blew out a heavy breath. "Fine. I'll talk to Karen, but that's all I'm promising you for now."

Mandy was right about one thing: since Mary's death, she'd been thinking about pushing herself beyond her comfort zone.

Mandy threw her arms around Lauren's shoulders and squeezed gently. "You won't regret it, Laur, I promise."

Lauren laughed softly. "I sincerely hope not."

* * *

Lying in the darkness of her bedroom, Lauren stared at the shadowy ceiling above her. A glance at the clock told her it was just past nine. She needed to be sleeping. After all, she had to be up at three, so she could be at the bakery by four. But no matter how many times she closed her eyes, sleep wouldn't come.

All because she'd gone over to see Trent tonight. Steph's casual mention of him two nights ago had inspired the worry.

For the longest time after he'd come home, Trent's PTSD had meant he'd barely left his apartment, even to fill his fridge. It's what had worried his family so much and why she'd taken to going over to see him on a regular basis. She'd wanted to help. A decision to bring him food one night had launched a thousand arguments and a thousand conversations.

Over the last year, he'd become a friend. She'd gone over to check on him one night after work, nine months ago now. Bringing him meals he could keep in the fridge and heat up later had always just been an excuse. She'd expected him to be his usual grumpy self, that he'd glare at her and tell her to leave. It's what he always did. She'd barge into his apartment—because she'd been instructed not to take no for an answer—and he'd follow her around as she made him a meal or cleaned and complain about her "invading his damn house."

This particular time, though, he'd actually invited her to stay. Ever since, it had become a tradition. Once or twice a week, she'd take him a meal or two, and he'd invite her to have dinner with him.

So it had been when she'd gone to see him after work today. They'd sat and chatted about their days while chowing down on the lasagna and garlic bread she'd brought over.

Now, hours later, she couldn't sleep because she couldn't stop seeing his smile. Being a serious man, he didn't smile often, but when he did, he was downright magnificent. It transformed his whole face. Harsh, cut features softened, and his cobalt-blue eyes lit up like the sun.

God, she swore she'd gotten over her crush on him in high school. After all, he'd gotten married and had gone overseas, and she'd grown up and moved on. But since he'd come home, those scintillating feelings had begun to sneak up on her again. Except Trent was now divorced. Single. And that solitary fact teased her senses. Her body didn't seem to care that he tended to treat her like she was another sister. That he didn't seem to see her as a woman.

No, she always came away from time with him more aroused than she knew what to do with. Trent was every woman's dream.

Polite. Charming. Funny. A hard worker. And it all came in a rock-hard package. God help her, he'd become her naughty little secret.

Even now the addicting rumble of his laugh echoed through her mind, shivering down her spine and landing straight in her panties. He'd teased her about her need to clean whenever she came over. It had started as an excuse to stay, to force him to interact, but had long since become a nervous habit.

Tonight he'd bumped her shoulder and laughed, and that one simple contact lit her body on fire. Because lately she couldn't help imagining what that hard body of his would feel like pressed against hers.

Giving in to the pull, she closed her eyes and slipped her hand inside her panties. Already hot and wet, a single glide over her swollen clit sent a heated shiver running through her. Her breathing hitched as her mind filled with the now familiar fantasy. Her favorite. The heat of his body against hers. His hot mouth skimming her neck, her shoulder, her ear. Teasing her sensitive skin. He'd slip those wonderfully long, warm fingers into her panties, massage her aching clit.

It was so real, she swore she could feel the hot huff of his breath in her ear. The calluses on the tips of his fingers. All too quickly, the luscious, achy pressure built. Heat prickled along her skin, and her inner muscles began a rhythmic squeezing, tightening and loosening. She rocked her hips into her hand, all the while imagining her fingers were his. Massaging. Circling. Driving her out of her mind with their ability to send her careening toward bliss at breakneck speed.

It didn't take long. Just the thought of him had made her so hot a few flicks over her engorged clit pushed her over the edge. Her orgasm tore through her, a luscious, hot bubble that burst inside of her. She massaged through every blinding pulse, determined to make it last as long as possible.

When the luscious spasms finally subsided, she collapsed back onto the bed and opened her eyes, lying there a moment, limbs deliciously heavy, while attempting to regain control over her breathing. The shadowy ceiling came back into focus, and the quietness of the house seeped around her.

The unbearable loneliness crept up right behind it. The way it always did. The one thing missing in this scenario was the warm, masculine body against her side. She longed for the pleasure to have been shared and for strong arms to hold her while she slept, and their lack left an emptiness deep inside.

Now, staring up at her ceiling, all she could see were the similarities between her and Mary. Mary had been a sweet woman with a heart of gold. She'd given Lauren a good life and had made her feel loved. But Mary had never been willing to take risks, had never put herself out there. And then she'd died alone, never having found her true love. What if Lauren ended up the same way?

Determination expanded inside of her. She pulled her hand from her panties and moved into the attached bathroom. After relieving herself and washing her hands, she strode down the hallway and into the kitchen. There on the counter sat the notepad she wrote her grocery list down on. She pulled it close, grabbed the pen beside it, and started making a list of all the things she'd never done but had always wanted to.

1: Lose my virginity

She paused, frowning down at the pad. Accomplishing number one would require finding the guy first, though.

Her conversation with Mandy two evenings ago came flooding back.

Go talk to Karen and decide for yourself, she'd said. *You shouldn't lose your virginity to some jerk you meet in a bar.*

Mandy was right. If she really wanted to lose her virginity, she needed to put herself out there.

She turned back to her list, making another note.

2: Call Karen at Military Match.

* * *

Lauren eyed her image again in the full-length mirror beside her dresser. A week had passed since she'd made the decision to call Karen at Military Match. Tonight was her first date. Turned out Mandy was right. Talking to Karen had all but made the decision to sign up easy. The woman had impressed her. Karen had a firm vision for her business, one with her clients' needs at heart.

Over the last week, as she'd waited for tonight to arrive, she'd also added a few more things to her list. She wanted to make out with a guy in public, and she wanted to get drunk. Just once. After all, wasn't that what college kids did? She hadn't, and she wanted to know what it felt like.

She'd also made a decision about tonight's date. She had every intention of checking off a few items from that list, and if she was doing this, then she was going all in. Tonight she was going to seduce her date. Have a hot fling for the first time in her life with a decent guy.

She'd need help, though. She hadn't a clue what to wear, and she was so nervous she couldn't stand herself. So she'd called Mandy and Steph for help. She'd planned her entire day so that she wouldn't have to worry later. She'd gone to the bakery extra early this morning to make certain all their orders were filled and the shop's shelves were packed. She'd left Lauren's Chocolates and Pastries an hour earlier than usual, so she'd have extra time to fret over what on earth to wear.

When she got home, Steph and Mandy waited on the porch, arms loaded. God bless her best friends.

Now, an hour later, Mandy had taken care of her hair and makeup. Steph had brought over the wardrobe. Mandy, at least, hadn't gone over the edge. She'd dolled up her usual perfunctory makeup and forced her to take her hair out of the ponytail she usually kept it in.

Steph, however, had gone completely crazy. Tonight's outfit was something Lauren wouldn't normally have been caught dead in. The zebra-striped blouse Steph had chosen lay open down to the button between her breasts. The V of the thin black sweater overtop was cut almost to her belly button. The black jeans at least she was comfortable with, but they were tighter than she would have preferred.

She turned to frown at Steph in the glass's reflection. "Are you sure this is the right look for tonight?"

"You're just lucky I decided to let you wear jeans and not that skirt I brought over." At Lauren's frown, Steph looked up, meeting her gaze in the mirror. "You want to get laid, right?"

"Yes, but…" Lauren eyed her reflection again. As a divorce attorney for a local firm, Steph was the more adventurous and confident of their trio. She had no qualms about wearing something formfitting and low cut, and she had the perfect hourglass figure to pull it off. Lauren, however, had always been tall and gangly and just this side of awkward. She'd *never* worn something so risqué.

"Uh-uh. No buts." Steph frowned in admonishment. "If you want to get laid, babe, you're going to have to leave behind your schoolmarm wardrobe. I still think you should've gone with that skirt instead of these jeans. Show a little cleavage and a little thigh and he'll be following you around like a lost puppy."

"We're just meeting for coffee. It's not like we're going to a club or anything. That skirt was way overdone." And too damn short for her tastes. "You realize I'm going to break my ankle in these heels, right?"

The heels *were* gorgeous, and they *did* make her legs look awesome. She *felt* sexy. Her and heels, though, had never gotten along well. More than likely she'd trip over the sidewalk and fall flat on her face. As usual.

"Well, you look smokin' hot." With one last small adjustment to the thick brown leather belt around Lauren's waist, Steph smiled in satisfaction. "You've got a great body, hon. You just need to learn how to show it off."

And that right there was the flaw in her little plan. She wasn't comfortable baring her assets to the world the way Steph was. She had too many memories of watching her mother get dressed for one of her dates. She eyed her reflection again and sighed. But wasn't stepping out of her comfort zone the whole idea of this?

Mandy appeared beside her in the mirror and looped an arm around her shoulders. "He won't know what hit him."

Knowing that, however, did nothing for the nauseated sensation swirling in her stomach. She had one too many memories of guys promising to call but never actually doing it. If she didn't hurl on her date's shoes or fall flat on her face, it would be a miracle.

* * *

Trent Lawson paced the sidewalk along the windows of the Starbucks. He scanned the street around him as he walked, his heart hammering from the vicinity of his throat. For the first time in almost twelve years he had a date.

This wasn't where he'd seen himself the day he married his now ex-wife. Wasn't where he'd seen himself when he'd come home eighteen months ago with his shoulder blown out, his leg in pieces, and his mind scattered to the wind, either. Hell, he still wasn't a hundred percent. He was still healing, still getting a handle on his PTSD, and his triggers were everywhere. Just last week the pop of a child's toy gun had sent him into a tailspin. He'd hit the ground before realizing it wasn't real. He still woke most nights covered in sweat from nightmares about the brutal things he'd seen overseas.

How the hell could he support someone emotionally when he was still drowning himself? But he missed the warm body beside him in bed at night. So here he was, standing in front of a coffee shop, divorced and waiting on a woman whose name and face he didn't know.

That was supposed to be *fun* part of the dating service he'd signed up with a month ago. He'd gotten the name of the place from one of the guys he worked with. Gabe Donovan and Marcus Denali co-owned the custom bike shop where he worked. Fellow SEALs, the guys had become his good friends since he started there six months ago. Who else but a fellow vet could possibly understand his aversion to large crowds and loud noises?

Gabe and Marcus had a firm business rule: they only hired vets. A month ago Gabe hired Mike. Mike was army, and his wife, Karen, owned the premier matchmaking service Military Match. Which was how he'd come to find himself here. Mike could talk the Pope into going to a strip joint and had convinced Trent to give Military Match a try.

When he'd woken in the hospital a year and a half ago, he'd promised himself he'd do everything the guys who died that day in the desert couldn't—he'd live his life. He wanted...Hell, he didn't even know. To date. To go out and have a little fun. Getting laid might be nice.

Everything he currently wasn't doing, which was why he'd signed up with Military Match. It went a long way that the place had a good reputation. They took care of the arrangements, and you simply showed up. And it was only coffee. Not drinks or a big, fancy dinner, so there was no pressure. It still meant he had a blind date, though.

He dragged a frustrated hand through his hair and turned to scan another direction. He was supposed to be keeping an eye out for a brunette wearing blue. The problem was, a dozen brunettes had passed him since he'd arrived ten minutes ago. On top of that, it being a spring evening in Seattle, it was barely fifty degrees out and, of course, drizzling. How was he supposed to see what she wore when everyone passing him all wore coats and hats? Unless his date showed up wearing a freakin' sign on her chest, he hadn't a clue how he'd recognize her.

She could be any one of the women seated at the café's outdoor tables.

Hell. He'd no doubt keel over before she ever got here.

He turned again to pace the other direction when a sight stopped him cold. Twenty feet away, a woman stood at the other end of the building. Hands tucked in the pockets of her black coat, she seemed to be waiting. Her head moved as if she scanned the crowd around her. Although he only had the back view of her, he'd long since learned to recognize the slender length of her body.

It was the curve of her tight little ass, however, that sealed the deal. He'd spent the last year trying not to notice how incredible that ass looked in a pair of worn jeans. Never mind that the ones she was wearing right now were fitted to her body, showcasing incredible curves.

Lauren Hayes. His heart hammered as his gaze zeroed in on the peacock-blue scarf peeking out from beneath the collar of her coat. Like a neon freakin' sign, it shouted at him.

Shit. If she was his date tonight, he was screwed. Lauren was his baby sister's best friend, not to mention she was ten years his junior. That made her strictly off-limits. He'd known her long enough to watch her go from a gawky preteen into a beautiful woman. He hadn't noticed exactly *how* beautiful until after he'd come home. After she'd spent hours at his place, cooking for him, helping him clean…and forcing him to get up and live.

God. What the hell would Mandy say if she found out he had the hots for her best friend? Hell, who was he kidding? She'd probably be happy he was at least dating someone. Not that he intended to give in to his attraction. She was still off-limits as far as he was concerned, which meant whatever he felt for her would be quashed.

Telling himself that didn't stop his gaze from caressing the curve of her ass again, though. Or his cock from leaping in his jeans, reminding him how long it had been since he'd last had sex. Not quite two years. He and Wendy had made love the night before his last deployment. Six months later he'd gotten her *Dear John* letter, telling him she'd fallen in love with someone else and she was leaving him. The price of being married to a Navy SEAL who was often gone for ten months at a time had been too high for her. He'd come home in pieces to divorce papers waiting for him.

He eyed Lauren again. Shit. He couldn't stand here all night gawking at her or he'd never find out whether she was his date or not.

He approached from behind and leaned his head over her shoulder. "Fancy meeting you here."

She started and whipped around to face him, eyes wide, but wobbled on her four-inch platform heels and pitched sideways. He grabbed her elbow to help steady her, and her hand caught the lapel of his jacket, gripping it tight. When she steadied herself, she let out a sigh of relief.

He chuckled and darted a glance at her shoes. "You're going to kill yourself in those things."

She furrowed her brow and swatted his arm, but the corners of her mouth twitched. "Because you scared the hell out of me."

"Sorry. Saw you standing over here and thought I'd come say hello." He let his gaze trail over her, taking her in from head to toe. "I was going to ask if you were just leaving the shop, but clearly you have a date. You look great."

Lauren was a button-down shirt and worn jeans kind of girl. He'd never seen her in anything quite so revealing. Her top hugged the contours of her slender shape, the low neckline teasing him with a view of her cleavage but not so much she spilled out of it. It was all he could do to keep his eyes on her face. That was more of Lauren than he'd ever seen.

"Thanks." She released his jacket and glanced down at herself. "I feel ridiculous in these heels. They're Mandy's, and she insisted they're sexy, but damned if I can walk in them."

He scanned the length of her legs, from the shoes up. "She's right. Those heels on you *are* sexy. That top is stunning."

Her gaze snapped to his, eyes wide and stunned. Yeah. He shouldn't have said that, but a soft flush rose in her cheeks, and her lashes fluttered as she diverted her gaze to the ground. A worthwhile reward for having said far more than he ought to. Lauren could be bold as brass when she wanted to be, but sometimes, like now, he caught sight of a more innocent side of her.

That softer side drew him like a bee to a bright yellow flower. That natural innocence made her shy, and he'd long wondered what it would take to bring down those walls. Who she was when she wasn't holding herself back. He'd bet his every last dollar that behind her shy facade lay the heart of a passionate woman.

He darted a glance around. "So, where's your date? He didn't stand you up, did he?"

The flush in her cheeks deepened, and she let out a heavy sigh. "I wouldn't know. He could be standing behind me, for all I know. I have a blind date. We're supposed to meet here, and I'm supposed to be looking for someone in blue."

His heart stuttered to a stop. Son of a bitch…

He tucked his shaking hands in his pockets and prayed, somehow, it was only a coincidence that they were in the same place at the same time…waiting on dates wearing blue. "Let me guess. You weren't given his name, only a vague description. You were told where and when to meet, and to wear something blue so he'd recognize you."

Her brow furrowed, those big brown eyes searching his in confusion. "How did you…?"

He swallowed a miserable groan. Fate was a cruel bitch. "And the woman who set you up, her name was Karen?"

Lauren's throat bobbed as she swallowed. "Yes…."

Of all the women to find himself set up with. Though he couldn't be sorry it was her. If he had to spend the evening with someone, it might as well be someone he was comfortable with. And he *was* comfortable with her. When he'd come home in pieces a year and a half ago, he'd wanted to be left the hell alone, to heal and deal with his shit on his own.

His mother and Mandy would have none of it. They'd insisted on caring for him, refusing to let him sit and wallow. Lauren had offered to help and had become part of the almost daily routine. She'd brought him meals, things she'd taken the time to make from scratch. Despite that he'd bitten her head off more than once, she'd sat with him. Sometimes she'd babble at him, filling him in about her day or complaining about the ceaseless rain. Sometimes she sat with him in silence, watching TV with him.

He couldn't pinpoint when exactly his feelings for her had changed, but she'd become a friend. One he treasured. Just being near her soothed his ragged nerves.

All it meant was he had a date with the one person he shouldn't touch with a ten-foot barge pole. He wasn't sure he'd healed enough to handle everything that came with a relationship, and Lauren…deserved better.

Now he had to tell her he was the date she'd been waiting for, and he hadn't a damn clue how to break the news to her. So he stuck out a hand and winked. "Hi. Trent Lawson. I believe I'm your date."

CHAPTER TWO

Lauren clenched her jaw to keep it from hitting the pavement. For a long moment, she could only stare at Trent's outstretched hand. Was he serious or playing a cruel joke? The light blue color of his buttoned-up shirt suggested he was telling the truth. Her date was supposed to be wearing blue. But the color was common for this type of shirt. It could just be a coincidence.

Except Mandy *had* mentioned that Trent knew Karen. What Mandy distinctly hadn't told her, though, was that Trent had signed up with Military Match, too.

She lifted her gaze to his. "*You're* my date?"

Trent dropped his hand and glanced at the sidewalk, going silent for a moment. He'd changed since coming home. He'd always been a man of few words, but that side of him had grown since he'd gotten out of the service. He often drew into himself, as if his mind had wandered. Part of his PTSD, Mandy had told her once.

That wasn't all that had changed, though. The military crew cut he'd worn for almost forever had grown out. His hair was now long enough to run her fingers through. He also seemed to be keeping a day's worth of growth on his jaw. Scruff looked good on him. The black leather jacket, however, he'd had since she'd first met him. It was well-worn and soft.

Just as she wondered if she'd have to pull him back from his memories, Trent tucked his hands in his pockets and looked up at her again. "Looks like it. I was told the same thing, to meet my date here. So far you're the only brunette I see wearing blue."

What were the odds of that happening?

Her conversation with Mandy came rushing back. *"I know a hot military guy who'd be right up your alley…"*

The little rat had done it anyway. Mandy had signed her up for this stupid dating service knowing her brother had signed up, too, then played matchmaker.

Lauren folded her arms and diverted her gaze to the building on her right, praying it was too dark for Trent to notice her scorching cheeks. This didn't get any more embarrassing. "I'm going to *kill* your sister."

Trent's brow furrowed. "What does Mandy have to do with this?"

Lauren dropped her arms. "She's the reason I'm here. Military Match was her idea. She signed up the three of us, me, her, and Steph, and told me about it afterward. Clearly, she set me up"— she waved a hand in Trent's direction—"with you."

Trent studied her for a moment, blue eyes searching. Seconds later, his features sobered. "She couldn't have."

If she wasn't so damned embarrassed, Lauren might have laughed at the irony. She'd have to fill him in. Of course, she *could* lie her way out of this, but she *never* ran from a fight. She believed in facing what God set in her path. Mary had taught her that.

Swallowing her pride, she sent up a silent prayer the right words would appear in her mouth, that he wouldn't laugh in her face or she wouldn't puke on his shoes.

Heart hammering like a freight train, she forced herself to hold his gaze. "She could have and it looks like she did. She knows I had a huge crush on you in high school."

She pulled her shoulders back and waited. Yup. If that didn't seal the deal on her humiliation, she didn't know what would.

Trent didn't react at all the way she'd anticipated. He smiled. Damn him. "I know."

Her stomach rolled with nausea, and Lauren folded her arms. The gesture made her feel stronger at least. Not so much like she wanted to melt into the sidewalk. "Of course you do."

He let out a quiet laugh. "Sorry, but you weren't very good at hiding it. I'd look at you and you'd blush to the roots of your hair, then giggle. Lord, you two did a lot of giggling when I was around."

The heat in her cheeks deepened, until she was sure her whole head had caught fire. God, it didn't get any better than this. Having powers of invisibility would be fantastic right about now.

Desperate to play it off, Lauren waved a dismissive hand at him, but couldn't bring herself to meet his gaze. "It was the military thing. Guys in uniform have always done it for me."

Apparently not done tormenting her, Trent nudged her arm. "What, you mean it wasn't my charming personality?"

Lauren met his gaze. Trent's eyes gleamed with playful impishness, and everything south of the equator liquefied. No way could she let him get away with teasing her, though. After all, she was here to get laid, right? Who better to practice her flirting on than a man she could never have? She and Trent were just friends. No doubt he'd laugh again and they could dismiss the whole notion.

The sooner he did, the sooner she'd stop feeling like she'd just told him she was from Mars, and the sooner they could get back the comfortable companionship they'd developed over the last year. Okay, so deep down, it wasn't what she wanted with him. Not really. Spending time with him often left her feeling caught between a rock and a hard place. Knowing he thought of her as little more than another sister was painful at times, but it was better than nothing.

She let her gaze trail over him. "Nope. Definitely the uniform. You looked pretty hot in yours."

There, let him chew on *that* for a while.

Trent tipped his head back and laughed. Despite knowing he laughed *at* her, the deep, husky sound still lit up her insides, shivering all the way down her spine and straight into her panties. She'd always loved that sound. Trent didn't laugh often, but when he did, every pair of panties within a two-block radius melted. Hers included.

Before she could do much more than react, Trent grabbed her hand and headed for the Starbucks entrance. "Come on. Let's go get some coffee. We're here. Might as well enjoy the evening."

Too stunned by the feel of his hand in hers, all rough and workworn and so damned warm, Lauren stumbled after him like a lovesick puppy.

Several minutes later, they sat inside at a small, round table by the front window. A little after six p.m., the sun was dipping below the horizon, darkening the already dreary day. The sidewalk around them teemed with people, coming and going about their evenings.

Across from her, Trent sat back in his seat, his gaze set on her. He'd been studying her for a good minute now but had yet to say anything. She could *see* the wheels of his mind turning in the way those intense eyes searched hers. It drove her nuts, because she'd kill to know what he thought. She'd admitted to having a crush, but somewhere over the last few minutes, while standing in line and ordering coffee, Trent had retreated into his head. As usual.

Finally, he set his coffee cup on the table. "Can I ask you a question?"

She plunked her chin in her hand. Hell, at this rate, she really would be a virgin until she died. "Oh, yeah, sure. Ask away."

"Why do you even need a dating service, anyway?"

Lauren rolled her eyes. "Yeah, like I'm the catch of the county. See the men waiting in line behind me?"

Trent blinked at her. "I'm serious. You're warm, and you have a great sense of humor."

Lauren laughed. "Trent, that's what you tell a woman you find ugly. You lie, to spare her feelings, and tell her what a *great* person she is."

Trent dropped his gaze to his cup. "You'd be surprised how many men I served with who just wanted a nice girl to come home to."

She waved a hand at him and sipped at her coffee. "Being nice is highly overrated. I'd rather be drop-dead gorgeous. Like Skylar. Now, there's a woman with a perfect figure, and she's forty-two."

Trent's twin brother, Will, was engaged to a woman five years older. Skylar was smart, the CFO of the telecommunications company the two worked for. She was a perfect size six, with curves where they were supposed to be. She was sweet as Southern iced tea, but Lauren always felt about as attractive as a light pole next to her.

Trent lifted a brow. "Who says you aren't drop-dead gorgeous?"

Lauren scoffed. "Oh, I don't know. Every man currently not beating down my door. Every date I never heard from again."

His coffee cup paused halfway to his mouth. Trent blinked at her like she glowed toxic green.

Lauren narrowed her gaze at him. Despite the chill in the air, she sweltered beneath her sweater and coat. "And if you tease me, I'm going to beat you over the head with my purse."

This whole conversation was nudging her insecurities. The geeky virgin nobody seemed to want. The owner of a bakery renowned for its beautiful wedding cakes who had yet to find a love of her own.

His stunned facade finally broke, a grin easing across his face. He sat forward, resting his elbows on the table. "Sorry. I just have a hard time believing that."

"Oh, believe it. I could ask you the same thing, you know. Why the need for a dating service? Surely you of all people don't need help in that area." To cover the sudden flush rising in her cheeks, she winked at him. "SEALs are a hot commodity, according to Mandy and Steph."

Trent shrugged. "I needed a date for Will and Skylar's wedding. If I bring a *plus one*, Mandy won't try to fix me up, and believe me, she's looking forward to it. She seems to have taken it upon herself to find me a new wife." He rolled his eyes, one corner of his mouth hitching.

Lauren laughed. "Well, at least I'm not her only victim."

Trent chuckled and sipped at his coffee. "Forgive me if I'm not honored to be in the club. The dating service was a friend's idea. Will is the only one who knows I'm here, which is how I know Mandy didn't set this up."

She sighed. All she could be at this point was honest. What the hell did she have to lose? Her humiliation was already complete. "I chose that particular service because the woman who runs it has a good reputation for the kind of clients she accepts."

Trent nodded. "Karen makes sure her clients are all decent people. Yeah. That's why I used it as well. Even though it's a more serious dating site, not one of those apps for casual hookups, I'm not ready for a full-out relationship. Wendy…kind of took it out of me."

The mention of his ex-wife had the green-eyed monster rearing its ugly head. Funny how her growing crush on him had the ugly feelings cropping up. She'd never felt this way back when they were married. Now she couldn't deny she was jealous of all the things Wendy had had with him. Had and given up. Lauren dropped her gaze, muttering half to herself.

"Wendy was a bitch." When Trent laughed, she flashed him an apologetic smile. "Sorry, but she was."

Trent held up his hands and laughed again. "You won't get any arguments out of me. That's another reason why I used this particular service. I have far too much shit going on in my head right now. With my PTSD, I can barely take care of myself, so I'm not looking for something serious, which is what I told Karen."

His casual mention of his disorder had her mind shifting gears. Trent had come a long way in the last year, but he still tended to avoid crowds and public places. Which was why it surprised her he was here at all.

She reached out to touch him, needing to offer something, but thought better of it and pulled back, curling both hands around her cup. "Still have trouble, huh?"

One shoulder hitched in half-hearted fashion. He sat back in his chair and shifted his gaze to something behind her. "It comes and goes. I don't sleep much."

His gaze took on a faraway look, his eyes going glassy and unfocused, an expression she'd long since learned to recognize. Trent often got lost in his memories of the war. Was he lost now? Or just remembering? Recalling what his mother had told her about his disorder and how to gently pull him out it, she drummed her fingers on the table. "How's your leg?"

He'd broken the femur of his right leg in two places when an IED went off. They'd pieced him together with plates and screws, his mother had told her. She recalled months of physical therapy. To this day, he walked with a slight limp.

Trent's gaze returned to her. He blinked; then recognition dawned in his eyes. He reached beneath the table, and experience told her he was rubbing his right thigh. He did it often, though she'd never been certain whether it was a habit or because his leg still hurt.

"It aches when it rains. I'm looking forward to summer and a little dry weather for a change." A sudden grin broke across his face, and he pointed a finger at her. "You don't get off the hook that easily, you know. You never answered my question. Why use a dating service?"

She shrugged. "I want to lose my virginity before I'm too old to enjoy sex, and I'm kind of picky. I'd rather my first time be with a nice guy and not the selfish pricks I've managed to find. Mandy and Steph think I'm nuts, but...."

She let her words trail off as Trent froze in front of her. Like she'd told him she was from freaking Mars, he stared at her wide-eyed. "You're a virgin? At twenty-seven?"

Lauren rolled her eyes. Out of everything she'd told him, of course he'd focus on that. As if it were the most absurd idea he'd ever heard. Hell, it probably was.

She hiked her chin a notch, determined not to give in to the urge to shrink back and blush. Steph wouldn't. So tonight she'd pretend to be a little more like Steph. "I wasn't supposed to be after tonight."

He studied her for a long moment. Then his brows rose practically into his hairline. As if he'd suddenly gotten her none-too-subtle hint. "Wait a minute...Were you planning to seduce your date tonight?"

Another statement spoken like he couldn't believe it was even possible.

Deciding to grab the proverbial bull by the horns, she held his gaze. It didn't make her feel any less like she glowed toxic green, but she felt stronger at least. More fortified. "Right out of his uniform."

Tension moved over Trent. He jerked his head to the right, looking down the street, and mumbled something under his breath. She didn't quite catch what it had been, but it sounded an awful lot like, "Lucky son of a bitch."

Every inch of her tingled with sudden awareness. While some part of her brain told her to leave this conversation alone, the part of her that secretly crushed on him refused to let it go. Tonight was supposed to be about stepping outside her comfort zone. If she wanted to get laid, she'd have to learn to do this. Right?

So she stared at his profile, drew a deep breath, and sent up a silent prayer. "Excuse me?"

His gaze darted in her direction. He rubbed the back of his neck and shifted in his seat. "I said I find it hard to believe that you'd need to try so hard to have sex. If I were your date tonight, I wouldn't be able to keep my hands off you."

Her heart thumped a hopeful beat. Surely he hadn't admitted he was attracted to her?

God help her. She had to know. "You *are* my date tonight, and that's a non-answer. What if I told you I'm glad I ended up with you tonight? What if I made *you* that offer? What would you do then?"

Maybe it was the wrong thing to say to him, but hell, if she was going for broke, she might as well put it all out there. Maybe he'd do something really crazy and admit he was attracted to her, too. Or take her up on her indecent offer.

Trent turned his head, looking off down the busy street. "That's flattering, doll, but I'd have to turn you down."

When her heart sank into her toes she realized she'd spent the last few moments hoping. Seeing the impassive expression on his face made her chest hurt. Clearly she really was *just* a friend to him. The woman no man seemed to want. To hear it from him, of all people, only made it sting more. Maybe it was a stupid schoolgirl's crush, but it still stabbed at her heart to see the rejection on his face.

"Thanks for the coffee. I'm sorry I wasted your time." Too embarrassed to stay any longer, she pushed away from the table, wobbling her way toward the light on the corner. What a complete and utter disaster. Maybe she was better off as a virgin. No man to let her down at the end of the night.

Behind her, Trent let out a quiet curse, but Lauren ignored the sound and kept walking as fast as she could on what felt like stilts.

When she was halfway down the sidewalk, he darted in front of her, forcing her to stop. She made to sidestep around him, but he caught her arm and ducked down to look her in the eye. "What did you want me to say to that? You're my sister's best friend. Not to mention I'm ten years older than you."

She forced herself to hold his gaze, but her insides wobbled. "Nothing. Stupid me." Brows furrowed, she glanced down at his hand, glaring at his grip on her right arm. "Do you mind letting go of me?"

Trent let go of her arm and instead tucked both hands in his jacket pockets. He gave a slow shake of his head, remorse rising in his eyes. "I came home a year and a half ago with my head full of sand and feeling sorry for myself. Out of all the family and friends who barged into my life and insisted on helping me, you were the only one who didn't make me feel like a fucking invalid. You fed me, cleaned my messy-ass apartment, and sat with me, most of the time despite the fact that I told you, more than once, to get the hell out. And you didn't ask for a damn thing."

He lifted a hand, his gaze following as his fingers slipped through the ends of her hair, which had fallen over her shoulder. He was quiet for a moment, something melancholic and intense written in the lines of his face.

"I think you're an amazing woman, Lauren, and I think those guys who didn't want you were asshats. Don't let anybody tell you that you aren't beautiful. But I just can't risk hurting Mandy's best friend." He dropped his arms to his sides and straightened his shoulders. "I'm honored you thought of me, though."

Lauren rolled her eyes, because if she didn't at least pretend flippancy, she'd cry. She'd been rejected a lot in her life. Her mother had always been too busy with the men she dated. In school, she'd been that tall, awkward girl most guys tended to overlook. Since Mary's death, she'd been on so many failed dates she was starting to wonder if something was wrong with her. But this had to be one of her most humiliating moments. For the first time in her life, she'd put herself out there, stepped beyond her comfort zone.

Only to remember why she didn't.

A rejection from him stung more than the others. Maybe he'd always been a fantasy, something she secretly hoped for but knew would never really happen. But it had been *her* fantasy, and she'd cherished the "what if." And he'd just shattered it to dust by reminding her that he thought of her as little more than another sister. Reality unfortunately was a cold dose of ice water in the face.

"I'm just going to go." She sidestepped around him and stalked down the street. She wasn't sticking around to watch the whole date implode. Her already nonexistent self-esteem couldn't take the beating.

She bent down, yanking off the stilettos one by one and hooked them on one hand, then hurried down the cool, rain-dampened sidewalk to where she'd parked her car down the block. Trent didn't follow this time, and Lauren refused to look back. Never again. Men could go hang as far as she was concerned. Maybe she'd be a virgin until she died, but damn the lot of them.

CHAPTER THREE

T rent punched the doorbell and pivoted, pacing the length of Lauren's porch. The quiet squeak of a weathered board kept him company in the otherwise silent night. Lauren lived in a small two-bedroom house in one of the older neighborhoods in Bellevue. She owned a rambler with enough driveway to pull two cars in and enough porch to pace three steps each direction. This was a family neighborhood. The residents had long since gone to bed and the street beyond the house was peaceful.

He loved this place. It would make a good family home someday, and simply being near Lauren gave him the same sense of peace as his parents' house always did. It soothed an ache somewhere inside simply to stand on her damn porch.

He shouldn't have come. The last thing she needed was him rubbing salt into a wound, but he couldn't stop seeing the dejection in her eyes. The memory was another piece of shrapnel piercing his skin, jagged and painful and cutting deep. In trying to keep her at a safe distance, all he'd done was hurt her, and he hated himself for it. He'd gotten on his bike and come over, a deep-seated need burning in his gut to somehow fix this.

When no sound came from within the house, he stopped pacing and turned to stare at the door. Hell, he should leave well enough alone. No doubt she was already asleep. With a sigh, he turned and headed down the steps to the sidewalk. He got halfway to his bike, parked at the curb, when the slide of the dead bolt *chink*ing open sounded behind him.

"Trent?"

Fuck. He froze on the sidewalk and dragged a hand through his hair, every inch of him aware of her behind him. What the hell did he say to her? He ought to make an excuse, get back on his bike, and go the hell home. This was a bad idea all around.

"What are you doing here?"

He made the mistake, however, of turning. Lauren stood in the doorway in her pajamas. Blue flannel bottoms, of all things, and a white T-shirt. How the hell baggy, worn-out flannel could look so damn sexy on a woman, he didn't know. It didn't help that the soft light of the interior lent the whole house a warm, cozy glow that invited him in. His apartment was cold and empty.

He forced himself to face her. Feeling like an idiot, he tucked his hands in his jacket pockets. "I'm sorry. I probably shouldn't have come. I wasn't thinking about how late it was."

"It's okay. I wasn't sleeping." She dropped her gaze to her bare feet, flexing her toes upward.

The vulnerability that came over her caught him in the chest, and he was moving back up those steps before he could talk himself out of it. When he came to a stop in front of her, she lifted her gaze to his, those big brown eyes wide and so goddamn exposed.

"Are you okay?"

Of course she'd ask him that. Because she'd spent the last year and a half worrying about him. Taking care of him. She was the only one who didn't make him feel quite so...broken.

"I'm fine." He leaned his hands on the edges of the doorframe. If he didn't, he'd be crossing that threshold and taking her in his arms for the need to wipe the misery from her eyes. "I'm sorry if what I said earlier hurt you."

She let out a harsh laugh. "You came all the way over here at ten o'clock at night to tell me that? A text would have sufficed."

She was right, of course.

He let out an uncomfortable laugh. God, she was the only person in his world who made him feel this exposed, because she'd seen far too much of the stuff he didn't show many. The only person who knew him better was Will. The problem was, she didn't know it, and he sure as hell could never tell her. Because he was *trying* to keep a friendly distance with her.

She looked up and arched a brow in silent question.

Trent drew a breath for courage. *Start with the basics.*

"I couldn't sleep. Couldn't stop thinking about how we left things. I was halfway here before I even knew where I was going." He hitched a shoulder. The excuse was pathetic, but there it was.

"I'm listening." She folded her arms, holding his gaze with that boldness he'd always admired. Clearly she wouldn't give him an inch, and he couldn't blame her. She'd put herself out there tonight, and all he'd done was knock her back down.

He sighed. Straightened. Shoved his hands back in his pockets. "You surprised the hell out of me, you know. I hadn't expected you to proposition me. Hell, I'm not sure anybody's ever propositioned me."

She let out a sardonic laugh and turned her head, looking out toward the street behind him. "To quote someone I know, I find that hard to believe. For the record, it wasn't about you. I was prepared to seduce whoever showed up. I decided before I left the house tonight that what I needed was to step outside my comfort zone. I've spent far too much time hidden in the shadows. For once in my life, I was going to take what I wanted. You were…more like a test. To see if I could do it."

He wanted to laugh. If that wasn't Lauren in a nutshell. One of the bravest damn women he knew. Even in the face of the worst of his PTSD, when all wanted was to be left the hell alone, she'd handled him with care and kindness and strength. She had tenacity, and he admired the hell out of her for it. Except he couldn't tell her that, either.

He'd come all the way over here, though, to apologize. At the very least, he owed a version of the truth.

"Me too. Deciding to step out of my comfort zone, I mean." He leaned against the doorframe, peering past her into the house. The television in the living room was paused mid-image. "It's partly why I decided to go with Military Match. Finding a date to Will and Skylar's wedding was just an excuse. I've never been alone, you know that? I've always had Will. When I went into the service, I had the guys in my unit. Even over in Afghanistan, I was constantly surrounded by people. At the very least, I always had Cooper. When I married Wendy, I'd come home to her. Now it's just me, and I hate it."

She looked up, gentle understanding in her gaze. "Ever thought about getting a dog? You're good with them. You carry him with you." She nodded in his direction, gaze on his chest. Her words suggested she was staring at the tags hanging from his neck.

He reached up, fingering the familiar, warn metal. Grief twisted in his chest. He'd been a demolitions expert and a K9 handler, working with dogs trained to sniff out improvised explosive devices. He'd trained his two-year-old German shepherd, Cooper, from a pup. He'd spent more time with that dog than he had his wife. Cooper wasn't an animal but a partner. They'd lived together, ate together, played together. Cooper had relied on him for basic necessities, for companionship.

And Trent had gotten him killed. He'd failed his end of the bargain.

"No. I'm not ready for a dog. It still hurts too much." Trent shook his head and forced himself to release the grief, to focus on why he'd come. If he didn't, the guilt would suck him under. "My point being, I signed up with that service because I was looking for something in the middle. I wanted…someone to spend time with, someone who wouldn't attempt to pin me down. I figured I'd start with Will's wedding and see where it took me. I told Karen that when I signed up. I assumed she'd set me up with someone who wanted the same thing."

He'd never been the kind of guy who dated dozens of girls. He preferred his friends few but close, and he chose his sexual partners carefully. His divorce, though, had taken it out of him. He'd failed at love. He could blame Wendy all he wanted, but clearly he hadn't been a good husband to her. She'd felt enough of a loss in their marriage that she'd had to seek companionship elsewhere.

Lauren folded her arms, once again looking vulnerable and defeated. "Instead you got stuck with me."

Her quiet words were another arrow piercing his armor. Trent swore under his breath and pivoted, stalked to the stairs, and stopped on the top step. He fisted his hands at his sides and peered out at the darkened street around him, forcing himself to breathe through the overwhelming desire to yank her against him and unload everything he'd promised himself he'd never tell her.

She had no idea, not a fucking clue, how wrong she was. She'd blown his control to hell tonight by admitting she wanted him. Telling him she'd gone into their date prepared to seduce whoever she ended up with had filled his mouth with the bitter taste of jealousy. He couldn't stop thinking about it, couldn't stop imagining her in someone else's arms, and every image that filled his head made him want to put a dent in something.

He drew a breath, forcing his fists to unfurl, but couldn't bring himself to face her. If he had to look into those big brown eyes, he'd never get the words out. She made him too damn vulnerable. "That's just it. I'm not sorry I ended up with you. It's just ironic, really."

"Ironic that you ended up with someone who reminds you of your sister, you mean? I get it, you know. You're not attracted to me. Hell. So far, nobody is. So you can save your breath. I'm sorry I got angry. I was embarrassed, and it was a knee-jerk reaction."

This time the pain and dejection in her voice were sharp points piercing his insides he could no longer ignore. He pivoted and marched back to her. He ached more than he could ever remember to cross the threshold. To taste her. To just once hear what sounds she made in the heat of passion. To feel her body rise to his.

She was right. She needed someone who'd go slowly the first

time, who'd be gentle with her, and damned if he didn't want to be that man.

The thought of hurting her, of losing the easy friendship they'd formed, though, was a hole in his chest.

She stared at him as if waiting for a response, but what the hell could he say? She didn't remind him of his sister. At all. He just couldn't tell her that. Keeping her at a distance, as much as he hated it, was for the best. For her. Because Lauren deserved so much better than what he could give her at this point in his life.

Hurt flashed across her face, followed by an angry determination he knew all too well. Lauren hiked her chin a notch. "Well, as long as we're being honest, you really want to know why I made you that offer? In part because I was curious to know how you'd respond, but mostly? Because in the dead of night, Trent, when the loneliness eats away at me, do you know who I think about? You."

The stubborn glint in her eye told him that her bold suggestion was a taunt. No doubt in order to gain a reaction. Because the sweet, polite woman he'd come to know would never have said something like that in front of anyone.

Despite knowing all that, her words hit their intended target. Any and all blood normally reserved for important things like rational thinking rushed south. In two seconds flat, his cock thickened behind his fly. Knowing she thought about him in the dead of night shattered the last of his control. Blew it to hell and scattered the pieces all around him.

He was two desperate little seconds from dragging her against him when Lauren braced her hands on his chest, lifted onto her toes, and sealed her mouth over his. For a moment he could only remember to drag in oxygen. Her warm, lithe body against his shot his brain function to hell. Lauren wasn't wearing a bra. Her tightened nipples rubbed his chest as surely as if she were naked against him, teasing his skin and setting his blood on fire.

Christ, she tasted like heaven. Soft, pliant mouth. A hint of cinnamon. Her hands fisted the lapels of his jacket. To pull him in or shove him away, he didn't know, but she turned her head, slanting those luscious lips over his, and thrust her tongue inside, bold as brass. All those supple curves he'd admired from afar slid against the hard planes of his body, like she couldn't get close enough, and Trent lost his fucking mind.

More aroused than he remembered being in a long damn time, he wound his arms around her and dragged her closer before he even realized he'd moved.

A soft moan vibrated through her, snapping him back to re-ality. Trent finally found what little self-control he had left and pulled his mouth from hers. For a moment he could only stare at her. His heart hammered his ribs so hard he feared the damn thing would burst from his chest.

Shit. She'd gone and pulled that last punch, and he'd fucking caved. Like he had no self-control at all.

It didn't help that she looked as leveled as he felt. Her hot, harsh breaths whispered over his mouth, calling him back. Those big brown eyes drooped to half-mast and filled with a heat that burned through him.

She stared for one heart-pounding moment, eyes reaching and searching. "Don't stop."

For a singular moment, he contemplated taking her up on her offer, picking up the thread they'd started and continuing. But where would that leave them when it ended? Because it would. It had to. He just wasn't relationship material right now, and in the end he'd hurt her. And then he'd have lost her for good.

She was a bright spot in a dark world. He couldn't lose her. He wouldn't.

"Lauren…" Trent shook his head, released his hold on her, and backed away, but her fingers tightened around the lapels of his jacket, stopping his retreat.

She furrowed her brow and shook her head. "We're both adults. I may be a virgin, but I'm old enough and wise enough to make this decision for myself." She followed his retreat and pushed herself against him, sliding her hands up his back. "Stay the night with me, Trent. Be my first."

God she hadn't a damn clue how badly he wanted to.

He unwound her hands from his back and shook his head. "I'm sorry, but I can't."

Something that looked an awful lot like hurt flitted across her face before she straightened and folded her arms. Her features blanked. He'd seen the look enough times to know Lauren was shutting him out.

"Because I'm not your type. Yeah. I get it. Story of my damn life." With a slow, dejected shake of her head, she turned and started to close the door. "Go home, Trent."

Trent swallowed a curse, the taste of jealousy and possession bitter on his tongue. Somewhere in her statement was an asshole he ached to find and rip apart with his bare hands. He could let her think what she wanted. It would neatly sever whatever ties they'd formed tonight.

And they had formed them. He'd never forget her soft body against him or the taste of cinnamon in her mouth. Or how god-damn right she'd felt in his arms. Like she belonged there.

He drew a breath through his teeth and forced himself to remain where he stood, but neither could he keep the words from leaving his mouth. He couldn't tell her the whole truth, but he had to give her something. He couldn't remember the last time she'd been this angry with him, and he hated it.

He put his hand up, stopping the door just as it got halfway closed. "I can't risk hurting you, Lauren."

She halted. She didn't turn or even move to fully open the door again, but he'd take what he could get.

"The first time you showed up at my apartment, it had been a bad night. Too damn many dreams. Too damn many times waking up not knowing where the hell I was. And the crushing reality of remembering."

He reached up, fingering the tags around his neck again. There were three. His, Cooper's, and AJ's. Two of his team members had lost their lives because he'd made a fucking mistake. The youngest—AJ—had no family. No one to mourn him. So he'd asked to keep the young man's tags.

"I needed someone. Just to sit in the same room with me. To keep me grounded. Mom and Mandy mean well, but they hover and nag, and I just end up feeling pathetic. A shell of who I was. You take me as I am, even when I'm cranky as hell. I consider you a friend, Lauren. Friends are gold to me. I've lost far too many."

Lauren turned sideways to look at him. The curtains had fallen again, masking her emotions. With Lauren, it was always obvious. She was usually so open, so warm, that with her, when she shut herself off, an unnatural aloofness settled over her that always seemed wrong to him.

The smile she flashed didn't reach her eyes. "I'm honored.

Thank you for being honest with me. I'm sorry I put you in this position. You should go. I'm sure you have to get up early for work."

She didn't give him time to respond, but stepped back and shut the door, the snap of it settling into the frame loud in the otherwise silence of the night.

Trent turned and stopped for a moment, staring out at the darkened street, his heart in his fucking boots. If he'd done the right thing by keeping her at a distance, then why did it feel so awful? How come his gut was tied in a thousand sickening knots? He hadn't wanted to hurt her, but it seemed he'd done it anyway.

* * *

"Good afternoon, birthday girl."

The *ding* of the shop's bell chiming preceded the familiar voice, and Lauren turned her head, looking down the length of the interior. Mandy strode through the front door, Steph in tow. Both faces held bright—and mischievous—smiles.

A week had passed since her first date with Military Match. Since she'd gone and humiliated herself by not only propositioning Trent but kissing him. God, what a fiasco that had been. The whole evening had confused the life out of her. His rejections had stung, and she couldn't stop remembering his odd comments at the Starbucks, the subtle hints that he might be attracted to her, too. She'd finally decided she had to know. To stop being afraid all the damn time.

Except he'd turned her down again. Here it was, her twenty-eighth birthday, and not only was she still a virgin, but she was alone. Utterly alone in the world. So she'd called Mandy and Steph, admitted to feeling pathetic. They'd insisted the three of them go out for her birthday. But they were early. By several hours.

In the process of packaging up a dozen cupcakes for a customer, Lauren shot the two a smile. "Hey. I thought we weren't meeting until tonight?"

Mandy leaned her elbows on the glass countertop in front of her and winked. "That's what you were supposed to think."

Without a word, Steph moved around the counter to the doorway leading to the back of the shop. "We're here, Elise."

A high-pitched squeal erupted from the back room, where Elise, her assistant, was icing more cupcakes. It was Saturday, one of their busiest days of the week, and cupcakes were the item of the day. She and Elise had baked and iced more than two hundred this morning, but the display case was almost empty.

Elise exploded from the back room, a bundle of barely contained excitement. The joy on her face would've put the sun to shame. She all but ran around the corner, enveloping Lauren in a hug so tight Lauren squeaked in surprise. "Oh, you're going to have so much fun!"

Elise was in her midfifties, a plump little woman who loved what she did. She had the sunniest disposition Lauren had ever seen. Always smiling and laughing and chattering away. The customers adored her, and her cake-decorating skills were superb. Any other time, her enthusiasm made Lauren laugh. Now it had suspicion itching at the edges of her consciousness.

Lauren leaned back and narrowed her gaze on Elise. "What do you know that I don't?"

Mandy and Steph had been tight-lipped all week, hinting they had a surprise but refusing to share. It had her on edge. With these two, anything was possible.

Mandy straightened off the counter, her mischievous grin somehow widening. "That birthday surprise we told you about starts now."

Before she could ask what kind of surprise, Steph grabbed her arm and tugged her around the counter. "We're kidnapping you for the day, babe."

The young woman she'd been in the process of helping smiled. "Happy birthday."

Lauren laughed and shook her head. "Thank you. Hope your son's birthday is fantastic." She planted her feet, stopping on the other side of the counter, and turned a frown between Mandy and Steph. "Guys, I can't just leave the shop. We don't close until nine."

Elise, having taken over boxing up the customer's cupcakes, paused to wave her hands at Lauren.

"I've got the shop until Jean gets here at six. Lilly is coming in tomorrow morning to help me bake. The cakes for tomorrow are finished. All we'll need to do is bake for the day." Elise winked. "We got this. Go have fun. You deserve it."

"You heard the lady. Your job today is to have fun." Steph moved behind her, gripped her upper arms, and pushed her out the door.

The chime *ding*ed as Mandy pushed through behind them. "Thanks, Elise! You're a doll."

Elise's voice echoed from within the shop. "You just make sure that masseuse has muscles on top of muscles!"

Outside on the sidewalk, Lauren pursed her lips, looking from

Mandy to Steph. Never mind that they'd enlisted the help of her assistant. Neither woman even looked guilty about it. Nope. Mandy and Steph looked pleased with themselves. "Masseuse? What did you do?"

"First up is a day at the spa." Mandy grabbed her hand and tugged her down the sidewalk. "Then we're going shopping."

Steph winked at her as she fell into step beside them. "You're going to need something sexy for tonight."

Lauren planted her feet, turning to look between Mandy and Steph. "Wait. What's tonight?"

Mandy's gaze shot to Steph before returning to Lauren. Her eyes lit up. "We're throwing you a party! We rented out the Cypress Room at the Four Seasons. A live DJ and a professional bartender. I invited Mark and Scott, that gay couple whose wedding I planned last year? They're bringing their straight friends."

Steph winked. "And I've invited a few of the single lawyers in my office."

"Oh God, you didn't. I'm officially that pathetic friend." Lauren released a heavy breath and closed her eyes, exhausted by the prospect of the evening. "I don't know if I'm up for this, guys. I've had quite enough humiliation lately from the male persuasion. If one more man decides I'm not his type, I may just decide to join a convent."

Mandy squeezed her hand. "It's not a singles party. It's just a huge blowout. Because we can. Trent will be there. Will and Skylar and her sisters, Belle and Savannah are coming, too. It'll be a blast. You'll see."

Lauren laughed for Mandy and Steph's sake, but her stomach knotted. After her complete and utter humiliation last week, she didn't know if she was ready to see Trent again. How the hell did she act around him now? Did she blow it off? Pretend she hadn't propositioned him—twice—and he hadn't turned her down? That was the trouble. She wasn't sure she could.

Mandy tugged on her hand. "Come on. It's just a party. You deserve to have a little fun. Let your hair down for a change. But right now we're having a spa day."

CHAPTER FOUR

Trent peered out at the crowd before him. It was a little after eight, and the Cypress Room of the Four Seasons was jam-packed with bodies. The left side of the room, where he currently sat, contained a small buffet full of everything from finger foods to slices of birthday cake. A DJ's booth sat along the far wall. The majority of the people who'd come were all crowded in front of it, shaking and gyrating to the upbeat music. A fun, buoyant atmosphere pervaded the space and every person in it.

Everyone but him. The music bouncing off the walls throbbed through his skull, and the sheer number of bodies made him claustrophobic. Which was why he'd chosen to sit near the buffet. He was being a humbug, but he'd had to come. To show Lauren she was important to him, but also simply to see her, to be near her.

Lauren, however, appeared to be keeping her distance. A week had passed since the night he'd gone over to her place to apologize, but clearly she was still upset with him. She'd hardly glanced in his direction since he'd arrived an hour ago. The few times she had, her expression and had been cool and aloof. Would she even miss him if he left?

The problem was, he couldn't make his legs move. She mesmerized him. Out on the dance floor, Lauren was in the center of it all with Mandy and Steph. Wearing a long-sleeved black crop top that showed off her flat stomach and a pencil skirt that clung to her every blessed curve, she looked damn near edible. She wore heels again, these not so obnoxiously high, and God he loved her in them.

The light in her eyes held his attention. The smile illuminating her face seemed never ending. That four guys currently vied for her attention wasn't lost on him either. And yes. He was jealous. Damn it. His gut burned with the overwhelming desire to insinuate himself into the midst of them and proclaim her all his.

But she wasn't. He was *supposed* to be keeping his distance from her. Because he wasn't anything she needed or deserved. And she knew it, too, or she wouldn't be avoiding him. The problem was, he couldn't stop thinking about that phenomenal kiss. Or remembering her offer. What fool in his right mind turned down an offer like that from *her*? Chances were, she'd proposition one of those yahoos the same way and all he could do was watch.

The scrape of a metal chair over the hardwood floor announced he had company at the table. Skylar plopped down beside him with a breathless huff and sat back, staring at the crowd in front of her. "You know, you could just go ask her to dance."

The smile in Skylar's voice had Trent hard-pressed not to return it. Either she'd been talking to Will—who'd caught him ogling Lauren more than once—or he wasn't being as inconspicuous as he'd thought.

Trent sat forward to rest his elbows on the table, looping his hand around his untouched cup of soda. "Why? So I can show her I have two left feet? No thanks."

Skylar turned her head, eyes narrowed and lips pursed in disapproval. "So, you're just going to sit here and stalk her all night?"

Trent sipped his soda. Letting her think that was better than having to tell her he kept his distance because Lauren hadn't spoken two words to him since he'd arrived. Nor did he blame her for it. "I'm keeping an eye on her. That guy in the front keeps pushing drinks into her hand."

As he watched, one of the guys circling her smiled and tipped the end of her cup, all but pouring what was no doubt alcohol down her throat. The only thing that kept him in his seat was Mandy. She glared at the guy and shoved him off, then took the cup from Lauren and handed her a bottle of water instead. Who the hell had invited that guy anyway?

Skylar nudged his elbow. "Uh-huh. Sure you are. And it's her birthday. She's supposed to enjoy herself." She pushed to her feet, took his cup from his hand and set it on the table, then grabbed his elbow and tugged him out of his seat. "Come on. We're going to dance."

She didn't wait for his approval or denial, but dragged him toward the dance floor. Halfway there, they passed Will, a drink in each hand.

Will smiled. "Where are you two headed off to?"

Skylar paused long enough to take one of the drinks from Will's hand and downed it, then handed the cup back and pecked his cheek. "I'm giving your brother a shove in the right direction."

Trent shot his brother a frown and shook his head.

Will's grin widened. "Good. He needs it."

Once out on the dance floor, Skylar braced her hands against his back and shoved him in Lauren's direction. Then the rat turned to the crowd of men surrounding Lauren. Voice raised over the thumping, pulsing music, Skylar propped a hand on one hip. "So, boys. Who wants to dance with the bride-to-be?"

At forty-two, Skylar was a good ten years older than most of the guys surrounding her, but she was tall and blond and she kept herself in great shape. She had invites before Trent could manage to swallow his nerves.

Lauren's gaze pivoted to him. Her smile fell, reaffirming his earlier thought. She *was* still upset with him.

Fuck. That look on her face would make him do everything he shouldn't.

He held out his hand and flashed the brightest smile he could muster. "Any chance I can get a dance with the birthday girl?"

She stared at his hand for a moment before meeting his gaze and arching a cynical brow. "You sure you want to?"

He playfully rolled his eyes, grabbed her hand anyway, and tugged her close. She set her hands on his shoulders and swayed with him, but the stiffness didn't leave her body.

Trent sighed. He'd hurt her to the point she no longer felt comfortable with him. Hell, she wouldn't even look at him. Damn it. Somehow he had to fix this. "I didn't mean to hurt you. You have to know that."

"Don't worry about it. I'll get over it." Despite her statement, her tone held an aloofness that told him she'd put up walls against him. Big ones.

He'd have to be honest with her. There wasn't any talking around this anymore. He'd already gone and done too much. So he leaned his mouth beside her ear. He needed to be sure she heard every word, because he wasn't sure he could repeat it.

"I lost two friends that day. Watched them get blown to pieces. It was my job to find that bomb and I missed it. I got distracted by a couple of nearby children squealing. It was a split second, but it was enough, and I misread Cooper's cues. There wasn't just one bomb. There were three, all buried in the same area. I can't lose any more friends, Lauren. Especially you."

Heart hammering in his throat, he paused and waited for her to say something, to acknowledge that she'd heard him. It came seconds later. The stiffness left her body and she leaned into him. The move was subtle, merely a shift of her weight, but enough he'd felt it. Time seemed to stop. An entire room full of people fell away as his senses homed in on her.

Yeah. This was what he loved about being in her presence. She quieted the noise in his head. Trent closed his eyes, allowed himself to luxuriate in the moment, and kept talking, using the lull of her against him, her lean curves swaying to the beat of the music, and that sweet scent of hers to help him get the words out.

"Coming home was hard. It's not easy going from *that* to civilian life. Coming home to see life just went on. People went about their days like nothing happened. That's hard to adjust to. You don't come back the same. That shit etches itself inside of you. I'll carry those images with me forever. I go to sleep every night hearing their screams. Some nights it's the war in general that gets me. Hearing the constant gunfire going on around the base. To this day I can still hear the sobs of this little girl we found when we were clearing a building. Her entire family had been murdered by insurgents."

The images swirled in his head, bright flashes of things he'd give both his arms to forget. Or not to have seen at all. So he drew a breath and kept going, before he lost the nerve to say the words. Or the hell in his head sucked him under.

"When I need someone, you're there. No questions asked. No lectures. No fussing. I've lost far too many friends over the years. I don't want to lose you, too."

Lauren didn't say anything for so long he feared he'd simply pushed her too far, but after a moment she sighed and leaned her head against his cheek. "You okay with this crowd?"

The soft concern in her voice settled somewhere inside, filling him with a warmth he didn't know what to do with. It told him in no uncertain terms that she saw all those things he'd never meant to show her. Like he was made of clear glass. Which only made her that much harder to resist. Wendy had only seen the SEAL, the man in uniform. She'd had ideas about who he was, insisted he live up to them, and for a while he'd tried in a vain attempt to make her happy. Because he'd convinced himself he loved her. And he supposed he had.

She'd never looked at him the way Lauren had the other night, though. Which only served to fill his head with questions he shouldn't ponder.

He shrugged. "The music makes my head pound, but I'm all right."

She rubbed his chest, the warmth of her hand burning his skin through his shirt. "It's sweet of you to come, but you don't have to stay if it's difficult."

"And miss getting to dance with the birthday girl? Not a chance." Tempted to take her hand in his, or tug her closer, he forced himself to pull back enough to meet her gaze and smiled. "You look like you're enjoying yourself."

Her smile lit up her whole face. "I am. I decided tonight I was going to forget all my damn rules. After all, it's my birthday, and you only live once, right? I'm pretty sure I'm already drunk, but I haven't had this much fun in far too long."

"Well, you deserve it. I have something for you, by the way. It was too big to bring with me." The gift was probably lame, but his heart was in it at least. He'd picked up wood carving as a kid, using old sticks he found. His therapist had recommended he try it as a way to occupy his mind on those nights he had trouble. Turned out, his therapist was right. Carving gave him something to focus on and took him out of the painful memories.

Since he'd started spending a lot of time with Lauren, many pieces had been inspired by her.

Her brows rose. "Oh?"

"A birthday present. I'll have to borrow Will's car, but I'll bring it by tomorrow."

She studied him for a moment, something working behind her eyes. "Come over for lunch?"

"Sure."

She turned her head, gazing off to her right, the corners of her mouth twitching. "Good. You owe me a date anyway, since our last one got cut shorter than I'd hoped."

On some plane, he knew she was teasing, but guilt nudged his gut all the same. She was right. He did owe her. And then some. "I tell you what. How 'bout you come to *my* place. I'll cook, to make up for it."

"Deal." Her tone held smugness, but she leaned her cheek against his again and Trent forgot everything but the feel of her body swaying against him.

The song was woefully short, the soft romantic strains fading, replaced by an upbeat tune that thumped off the walls. As the couples around them disentangled, bodies once again surging to the new beat, he and Lauren stopped moving. Hands on his shoulders, she pulled back. The way she stared at him, the luscious tension rising between them, had him dreaming of *what if.* Namely, taking her up on her offer. Hell. Maybe a fling with Lauren was exactly what he needed to push him into the land of the living again. Into finally moving past the shit he'd seen overseas. God, he was tempted.

Lauren flashed a soft smile, and the warmth in her big brown eyes filled his soul. "If I don't see you again tonight, thank you for coming. It means a lot to me. I wasn't sure you would, all things considered."

Damn it. There it was. The soft side of her, the one that pulled at the lonely ache deep inside. He released his hold on her. If he didn't, he'd be pulling her back and attaching his mouth to hers.

Neither could he force himself to release contact with her entirely. Instead he cupped her chin in his palm, stroking her supple skin with this thumb. "We're friends. I couldn't *not* be here."

He'd hoped his words would finally soothe the wound between them, but Lauren froze in front of him. Her shoulders rounded as a palpable hurt filled her eyes.

"I'm really beginning to hate that word," she said, as if half to herself. "*Friends.* I tried to swallow my feelings earlier, because I appreciated what you shared with me. I know that's very painful stuff for you, and it can't have been easy to talk about it. But dancing with you, being close to you like this? I just can't pretend anymore that being your friend is really what I want. Because it isn't. I realize that kiss probably meant nothing to you, but it was something to me."

She pushed out of his arms and sidestepped around him, and

all he could do was watch her go. In trying to put her back in a safe place, all he'd done was hurt her. For the second time he had to ask himself, if he'd done the right thing, why did he feel like a complete ass?

* * *

A couple hours later Trent was still holding down the chairs. Lauren was still in the middle of that crowd, still surrounded by men, all seeming to hang on her every word. She was in fine form tonight. Clearly she'd meant what she'd said. She intended to enjoy herself. Though he wasn't sure he'd ever seen her quite *this* relaxed. She didn't seem like herself at all.

Some part of him told him he ought to go home, but he still couldn't make himself leave. He couldn't stop thinking about the last thing she'd said to him.

Those words haunted him. *I just can't pretend anymore that being your friend is really what I want. Because it isn't.* What she'd said next bothered him the most: *I realize that kiss probably meant nothing to you, but it was something to me.*

She was so very wrong. He didn't want to be that guy, another asshole on her list, but if he gave in to the desire burning through him, that's exactly what he would be. He couldn't give her forever. Oh, he knew Lauren would never do to him what Wendy had, but he wasn't sure he wanted a forever or believed in it anymore, and he refused to treat Lauren like a warm body. She deserved better.

Neither could he regret that kiss. For a moment he remembered what it was to be human again. That was the problem with being around her. He was addicted to the way she soothed his soul. Her words had kept him company for the last two hours, taunting him with what he wanted so badly his balls ached. To be her first.

The thought of her making love to anyone else, to one of these yahoos who could easily hurt her, had his gut tied in sickening knots and his hands curling into fists where they rested on his thighs. The images filled his head. Her bare skin and soft curves wrapped around someone who wasn't him. Her calling out someone else's name. Tension skittered along his nerve endings, and his right thigh began to bounce.

Will slid into the seat beside him, nudging him with an elbow and jarring him from his tangled thoughts. "How you holding up?"

Trent darted a sideways glance at his brother. "I'm okay."

At least he was in the regard Will was referring to. The shit in his head. The combat stress. Despite the crowd and the noise, Lauren kept him focused. Grounded. Like always.

"Are you?"

"I'm okay." He leaned over to bump Will's shoulder for reassurance.

Since he'd come home, Will had become overprotective, like everyone else in his family. With Will, though, it was different. They'd watched out for each other since they were kids, and because they knew each other so well, Will saw far more than anybody else. When Trent needed something or when something bothered him. Like now. No doubt Will had noticed his silence and tension.

Now, however, Trent couldn't resist the pull of a confidant. If there was one person in this world he could talk to without being judged, it was Will.

He looked over the crowd, watching Lauren. A slow song had

started, and some other guy had her in his arms. Which did nothing but give him a fucking visual to go with the tormenting images swirling in his brain. "Hypothetical question."

Will laughed. "They're never hypothetical."

Trent furrowed his brow but couldn't contain his grin. "Hypothetical question."

Will leaned back in the chair, folding his hands over his stomach. "All right. Lay it on me."

"Assuming you were single…if a woman offered you a night with her, would you take her up on it?" Truth was, he wasn't really a one-night-stand kind of guy. Down deep he was a home and family man. He craved a connection, not merely a warm body in bed beside him.

But with the divorce and the war still fresh in his mind, it was all he had to give. He had no desire to put his heart through the ringer again. Nor did he think he was capable of something more than fleeting right now. He could handle short term as long as it was on *his* terms.

Despite the nature of the question, Will didn't so much as flinch. "Do it."

Trent laughed, all sense of pretense gone, and looked over at Will. "You don't even know who she is."

Will shrugged, half-hearted and dismissive, and glanced over at him, his gaze somber. "Doesn't matter. You need it, bro. Mom and Mandy are right. You're isolating too much. It's not healthy. If she's caught your attention enough that you're even pondering taking her up on her offer, then follow wherever it leads."

Trent turned back to Lauren's form in the crowd. "Even if you considered her a friend?"

"Especially if she's a friend. It means she won't use you." Will pushed to his feet and settled a hand on his shoulder, his voice lowering. "She won't, you know."

Will's blatant statement told him in no uncertain terms he really wasn't hiding his attraction to Lauren well. Not that he should be surprised. He and Will never could keep anything from each other.

Except Will's acute observation had the confusion swirling in his head again. His overwhelming desire for Lauren warred with the need to hold on to her friendship whatever the cost.

"But I'd be using *her*." The knowledge settled in his chest like so much guilt, heavy and oppressive, reinforcing how wrong it was to take Lauren up on her offer. "I can't do that to her. I can't give her more than that, and I won't give her less. I've lost too many friends already. I don't want to risk losing her, too. She's a bright spot in the darkness."

"I know, but you can't stop living. At some point you have to get back up. For what it's worth, I think she's the perfect person to find your feet with. And if she made you that offer, then she knows what she's in for. Talk to her." Will gave his shoulder a supportive squeeze, then glanced at him. "You made any plans for the bachelor party yet?"

He sighed. When his brother had asked him to be his best man, Trent had been honored. Will was his when he married Wendy. Now, though, he didn't know if it was a job he was cut out for. His head wasn't in the game. "Not yet. I've been researching possibilities, but you haven't told me your preferences yet."

"Sorry. Work's been crazy. We're launching a new ad campaign, trying to get revenue up. Sky and I barely see each other these days, let alone have time to plan a wedding. She and I were talking a bit ago, though. We were thinking of a joint bachelor, bachelorette party type thing and forgoing the usual strippers and alcoholfest. This is her second marriage, and neither one of us is up for the custom unrestricted night out."

Trent could help but laugh. "Somehow I had a feeling you'd say that. I'm glad. We did that when I married Wendy and look how that turned out. I've been pondering things that didn't involve strippers. A tour of local breweries, maybe."

"Sky and I were thinking something like this would be great." Will nodded, indicating the crowd out in front of them. "Just a big pre-wedding bash with friends and family."

Trent nodded. "I'll set it up. Maybe I can set something up with a local brewery, have them bring in a beer sampler or something."

"Sounds good." Will studied the crowd out in front of him for a moment before drawing a breath. "Means a lot to me you accepted, you know. I know things have been hell since you got home, but I plan to get married only once, and letting someone else be the best man didn't feel right. It's been you and me from the beginning."

Trent leaned sideways, bumping Will's shoulder again. "From the womb, man."

Will nodded at the crowd again. "Heads up. Lauren's on her way out of the room, and she has a follower."

So he wasn't the only one who'd noticed Lauren's overeager new "friend."

Trent followed his brother's gaze in time to see Lauren round the corner out into the hallway beyond the room. Two steps behind her was the guy she'd been dancing with. The same one who'd been feeding her drinks all night.

Trent was on his feet and moving around the table before he could draw his next breath. "I got her."

Halfway to the ballroom entrance, Mandy moved into step beside him. "So you noticed him, too."

Trent grunted in response, sights set where he'd last seen Lauren. "Who the hell invited that guy? Do you know him?"

"I don't know. He must've come as someone's friend. I've asked him to back off more than once, but every time I turn around he's back, shoving more drinks into her hand. I told her she should let loose a little tonight, allow herself to enjoy the party, but that isn't what I meant."

"No worries. I'll make sure he gets a very clear picture." The thought had irritation prickling along his nerve endings and his hands fisting as his sides. He darted a glance at Mandy as they rounded the corner into the hallway. "But you should start winding this party down."

"Agreed."

As it turned out, they didn't have to go far. Lauren and her new "friend" stood outside the women's restroom, some twenty feet or so down the hall. She leaned against the wall, eyes full of fatigue. The guy had his hand braced beside her head. Even though she kept looking anywhere but at him and shaking her head, the asshole kept leaning in to her. Every time she pushed his hand away, it returned, grazing somewhere else he clearly wasn't invited to touch.

Trent ground his teeth and moved toward them. She'd hate him for following her, but the guy clearly wasn't taking no for an answer. He'd made it only halfway to her when Lauren braced her hands against the guy's chest and shoved with enough force he stumbled back two steps.

"I said no!" Her voice rang down the hallway, echoing off the walls.

Trent halted, unable to hide what was surely a smug smile. Even tipsy, Lauren wasn't helpless. Good for her.

"Atta girl," Mandy murmured beside him.

"You get her. I've got the jackass." Having seen enough, he resumed his trek in their direction.

Beating a hasty retreat, the asshole pivoted. As his gaze landed on Trent, he halted in his tracks.

Trent crossed the space between them, stepping close enough the guy wouldn't mistake his meaning. "You go back into that party, and I'm going break off both your arms and shove 'em up your ass."

The guy glared at him, but turned nonetheless and stalked toward the elevators.

Trent crossed to where Mandy now stood with Lauren and tucked his hands in his pockets. "You all right?"

"For the last time, you guys, I'm fine. I came out for some air and to pee, and he followed me." She shot a sideways glance between him and Mandy, eyes narrowed in irritation. "I appreciate the help, but I didn't need it. I *can* take care myself. I've taken self-defense classes."

His heart sank into his boots. Damn. He'd hoped she'd cooled off, that their chat earlier had somehow gotten to her, but clearly she was still upset with him. He ached to take her in his arms and cradle her against his chest. Or kiss her soft mouth. If only to make her stop looking at him like that.

None of which he could do, especially with Mandy standing right there. He still needed to clear the air with Lauren, though. He was going to fix his screw up or die trying.

He stuffed his hands in his pockets and looked over at Mandy. "Mind if I have a moment with her?"

When Mandy frowned, looking between him and Lauren in confusion, his gut knotted. *Way to go. Might as well just tell her you have the hots for her best friend.*

Scrambling to come up with a better reason, he quickly added, "I have a present for her, and I'd like to talk to her about a good time to bring it by."

Then he held his breath and waited. No doubt she'd see right through his lousy excuse.

To his complete surprise, though, Mandy nodded, then turned to touch Lauren's arm. "I'll be inside if you need me."

He waited, watching until Mandy disappeared into the ballroom again, before leaning against the wall beside Lauren. "I hate when you're mad at me."

Lauren didn't say anything, and tension mounted in the air between them. Just when he was sure she'd taken to giving him the silent treatment, her shoulders drooped.

"I'm not mad. I feel like a fool, truth be told." She pulled her lower lip into her mouth, gnashing at one corner, darted a glance at him, then blew out a heavy breath. "I should never have made you that offer."

"That takes courage, you know. To ask for what you want."

She let out a harsh laugh. "It's only courageous when the guy kisses you back. When he doesn't, it's just pathetic."

He *had* kissed her back. Had wanted to do a hell out of a lot more, too. Like slip his hands beneath her T-shirt for the need to feel her breasts. To hear her moan and sigh and shiver.

Not that he could tell her that, either.

Lauren dropped her gaze to her feet, wrapped her arms around herself, and shook her head. "That jackass you chased off didn't help any. It took me a couple of drinks to realize the *iced tea* he'd been getting me wasn't tea at all."

"Ah. Long Island Iced Tea. Wicked stuff." All alcohol, with a little cola for color and taste. When made the right way, the drink tasted exactly like tea and packed a hell of a punch because it went down like Kool-Aid. The asshole had fed her something he'd known damn well would knock a lightweight on her ass. Trent clenched his jaw. He should have decked the jerk while he had the chance.

"Exactly. When he followed me out here, I realized I was in over my head tonight. I wanted to have to fun, to let loose a little, and I have, but that jerk made me wonder what the hell I was doing. I'm not this person. I don't drink this much. I don't wear heels or dresses, let alone ones like this." She waved a hand over herself, indicating her outfit, then rolled her eyes. "And I can't flirt to save my life."

He wanted to tell her how wrong she was. Lauren didn't need to flirt. She had a warmth and realness about her that drew people, him included. When she laughed, it was honest and open, and any fool within miles turned to smile with her. "You seemed to be doing fine to me."

"Because I let Mandy and Steph fill me with false bravado. Alcohol helps." She let out a harsh laugh full of bitter self-reproach. "It's ironic, really. I decided two weeks ago I wanted to finally lose my virginity. That I'd step outside my comfort zone and live in the moment. That jackass would have gladly taken it, too, right there in the bathroom. I guess it just proves that at least *some* men are willing to sleep with me. Even if they are the wrong ones."

He jerked his gaze to hers, unable to hide the irritation sizzling along his nerve endings. "Did he tell you that? That he'd take you in the bathroom?"

"No. He invited me to his place, but he was so pushy I have no doubt had I invited him to do it in the bathroom, he'd have taken me up on it. Which isn't how I'd always envisioned my first time." She leaned her head back against the wall and closed her eyes, looking tired and defeated. "All I want now is to go home, but I hate the thought of disappointing Mandy and Steph. They went through a lot of trouble for me."

"Mandy's not upset. I think she's just worried about you. I can take you home if you want." He nudged her playfully with an elbow. "We can sneak down to the elevator before anybody realizes you're gone."

Lauren opened her eyes, her gaze soft but full of something he couldn't quite reach. She shook her head and shifted her gaze to something beyond him. "I can't ask you to do that."

He straightened off the wall and turned to her. "You didn't. I offered. And I don't mind. Think you can manage to stay on the bike?"

She let out a quiet laugh and reached up to rub her temples. "I seriously doubt it. The damn floor has slanted on me."

"I'll go get the keys to Will's Beamer. I'll just tell Mandy and Steph you're sick and want to go home." He touched her shoulder, then moved around her, heading back into the party.

CHAPTER FIVE

Lauren watched until Trent disappeared into the party room, then collapsed against the wall. She closed her eyes, fighting tears that wouldn't stop filling her eyes. Tonight had started out well and had gone straight to hell. The loneliness had settled deep inside the minute that handsy jackass finally walked away. Sadly, she couldn't even remember his name. Not that it mattered. Once again, she'd failed to find a nice, respectful guy. To top it off, it was her birthday, but she was still going home alone. The knowledge was eating a hole in her chest.

With a heavy sigh, she opened her eyes, willing away the self-pity, and straightened off the wall. She pushed into the bathroom. Never in her life had she drank this much. After Mary's death, she'd made a firm rule—she'd allow herself the luxury of a drink. After all, she was a normal, healthy adult. But her limit was one.

Tonight, though, she'd intended to get drunk. And she'd succeeded, which was why she'd switched to "iced tea" when that jerk had asked her what she wanted to drink. She'd just wanted to enjoy her birthday and not worry for once. Now she remembered why she'd made that one-drink rule in the first place. Too much alcohol clearly made her out of control, not to mention sick to her stomach.

Well, that was one item she could officially cross off her "things she'd never done" list.

After relieving herself and washing her hands, she exited the restroom. Trent leaned against the wall outside the door. He had one hand tucked in the left pocket of his jacket, her coat dangling over his forearm. The sight of him there tugged at all those lonely places. The scared little girl inside the supposedly independent woman, who'd kill to have someone to wrap around her at the end of the night.

And now the man taking her home thought of her as little more than another sister.

Before she could gather her wits, Trent straightened off the wall and held her coat open for her. "All set. I managed to convince Mandy and Steph you were sick and wanted to go home. Mandy was fit to be tied when I wouldn't let her come see you. I have strict orders to tell you that you're to call them both first thing tomorrow morning."

They walked in silence through the lobby, to where Will's car was parked in the center of the hotel's parking lot. Neither said anything during the twenty-minute ride across town to her place, either. She couldn't muster the energy to make chitchat, and he didn't push her. Trent seemed to retreat into his head, and for once, she was grateful.

After pulling up to the curb in front of her house and turning off the engine, he pulled out the keys and exited the car. He jogged around to her side, opened her door, and held out his palm before she'd even mustered the energy to sit upright.

He kept hold of her hand as he walked her to the door. He waited silently behind her while she dug in her purse for her keys, too, and after unlocking the door, of course he insisted on seeing her inside.

Standing in the foyer, she turned to him, but words wouldn't come. She had no idea what to say to him. His chivalry was doing her head in. He was the kind of man she'd envisioned when she'd signed up with Military Match in the first place. He was the complete opposite of that jerk he'd chased off earlier.

Trent reached out, thumbing her chin. "Will you be okay?"

The thoughtful, tender gesture shivered all the way down her spine and filled her chest with an ache she didn't know what to do with.

"I'm fine. Go home and get some sleep. I imagine you have to work tomorrow." She touched his arm in gratitude and turned, making her way toward the bedroom at the back of the house.

Okay, so it was rude to walk away and leave him standing there, but if she said anything else, she'd cry. The tears were too close to the surface. Of all the men she could have ended up with tonight, she'd ended up with the one she wanted the most. The good guy.

But he didn't want *her*. Trent considered her just a friend.

The one guy who *had* wanted her...had been a selfish jerk. Ironic, really. It seemed good men really did have no interest in her. It seemed her only hope was to settle for the jerks.

She waited until she heard the front door close before yanking off the top and skirt Steph had insisted she wear tonight. She'd managed to pull on her pajamas when the whole night caught up with her. She was totally and utterly alone in the world. And nothing proved that more than coming home to her empty house. Hell, maybe it was the alcohol. Wasn't it a depressant? But of all nights, tonight she needed someone. If only so she didn't have to sleep alone.

She sank onto the edge of the bed, flopped back, and gave in to the tears. Maybe if she cried it out, she'd get the hell over it. From the corner of her eye, she could see a large shadow filling the doorway. She rolled her eyes, her cheeks blazing, but didn't bother to wipe away the tears. Of course Trent had followed her. That was just like him. The Navy SEAL who'd risked his life for the freedom of others. Who held open doors for women and who carried the tags of the dog he'd lost in honor of his memory.

And here she was, bawling like a baby. What an impression she must be making on him.

She let out a shuddering sigh, a single tear escaping to roll down her temple. Christ, she had to be a mess by now. She ought to tell him to leave, but he'd been kind to her tonight, and she just didn't have it in her to put up walls against him. Ironically enough, of all nights, tonight she couldn't resist his friendship. She just needed *him*, even if only a friend, so that she wouldn't be so alone. "What's wrong with me, Trent?"

The bed dipped as he took a seat beside her. He lay back, his hand slipping into hers where it rested on the bed between them. "There's nothing wrong with you, doll. Some guys are just assholes."

Another tear escaped, but she didn't bother to wipe it away, either. "I seem to find an awful lot of them. Where are all the nice guys people are always talking about?"

He released her hand, lifting it instead to wipe the tears from her cheek with the pad of his thumb. "Where all the good women are. In hiding."

The hint of humor in his tone had her smiling in spite of herself. If he was going to think of her as only a friend, at least he was a damn good one. "You know what I actually hoped?"

"What's that?" He wiped more wetness from her cheek, then slipped his fingers through hers. He had big hands. Large and long fingered, they all but swamped hers. It was such simple contact, but his palm was warm and solid and right then it provided a lifeline.

"That I'd meet someone. Just one nice guy. Someone to curl up with me at the end of the night. I make wedding cakes for a living, yet I don't even know what it feels like for a man to look at me the way Will looks at Skylar."

He didn't say anything for so long she feared he wouldn't. She probably looked like a pathetic fool to him.

Finally, he squeezed her fingers and turned his head to look at her. "Want me to stay?"

She couldn't stop the derisive snort that left her. Of all the things for him to ask.

"How many times have you showed up on my doorstep and sat with me, even when I was too stubborn to admit I needed it? I'll take the couch."

Another damn tear slid to her hairline, the ache crushing her chest. Did he have any idea how much she wanted to scream yes? But she couldn't. She needed his friendship tonight, but she couldn't handle him sleeping in the house. It would only remind her too much of what she could never have.

"That's really sweet, Trent. It is. But you being on the couch would just be even more depressing, because it isn't what I really want." She hesitated. She shouldn't tell him anymore, but hell, what else did she have left at this point? "What I want tonight is someone to hold me while I sleep."

Trent went silent, simply staring at the ceiling. After a moment, he looked over at her.

"It's your birthday, and I'm in a generous mood. I also don't have anywhere to be tomorrow. Gabe's been giving me weekends off." He shifted their combined hands, nudging her thigh. "Don't go all shy on me now. Ask for what you want."

The lack of pity in his eyes told her he meant what he'd said. She ought to tell him no, but the word wouldn't leave her mouth. Maybe he was only a friend, but he provided more temptation than she had willpower to resist. "I'd like you to stay. To hold me while I was sleep."

He winked. "See? That wasn't so hard."

She let out a watery laugh and turned to stare at the ceiling. "I can't promise I don't snore."

"That's okay. If you don't, I'm pretty sure I do." Trent squeezed her hand, then pulled himself upright and stood. He hung his jacket off the bedroom doorknob, then returned to the bed. He pulled down the covers before moving back to her and scooping her into his arms. "Come on, doll. Let's get you into bed. You'll feel better after a little sleep."

She couldn't resist the warmth of his body or the pull of his familiar scent and rested her head on his shoulder. "Remind me never to drink again."

A quiet laugh rumbled out of him. "Somehow, I don't think I'll have to. That hangover you'll have tomorrow will do it for you." He laid her carefully on the bed and pulled the covers over her. "Stay there. I'll go get you some ibuprofen. Where do you keep it?"

She settled back on the pillow and closed her eyes. "Cabinet over the stove. Top right."

"Be right back." He was back a minute later, the bed sinking as he took a seat. "Here, doll. Sit up and take this."

She pried her eyes open, took the tablet from his open palm and popped it into her mouth. She swallowed it with a sip from the glass of water he'd brought as well, then set the glass on the nightstand. Trent returned to the doorway. He bent to unlace his boots and toed them off before flicking off the overhead light. Immersed now in darkness, his tall, broad form was little more than a moving shadow as he returned to the bed. He climbed in beside her, covered them both, and lifted his arm in invitation.

The thought of lying against that big, hard body had her heart doing a jig in her chest. It was so stupid, but she'd never done this before, actually *slept* with a man. It didn't help that her mind filled with his denial last week. *That's flattering, doll, but I'd have to turn you down.* Not to mention he was only here because he was a nice guy. Because she'd gone and cried and told him way more than she should have.

Her cheeks heated, and despite knowing he couldn't see her, she averted her gaze to the bed. "You don't have to do this, you know. It's kind of childish of me to ask this of you."

"It's not childish. Not even remotely."

His intense gaze bored into her, but otherwise, long moments passed in tense silence. She didn't have to see his face to know he'd retreated into his head. So she waited him out. He'd talk when he was ready.

After several moments, he released a heavy breath. "That feeling gets to me, too. My apartment is empty. There's no life there. Not even in me. Believe me. I understand the need. If all you want for your birthday is to be held, I'm happy to provide the warm body."

Knowing he understood made the decision easier. She scooted closer, tucked herself against his side, and rested her head on his shoulder, laying her hand on his stomach. His strong arm settled around her, drawing her tighter against him, and his hand settled over hers, clasping her fingers.

It was awful how right lying with him felt, knowing he didn't feel the same way about her. In the morning he'd leave and they'd go back to normal. Just friends. But for tonight he was solid and comforting, and she needed it. She needed *him*. Never mind he was still fully clothed, or that she knew this didn't have the same power for him as it did for her. His scent filled her lungs every time she drew a breath, and her whole body relaxed, the tension from earlier draining, lost in him.

"Trent?"

"Hmm?"

"Thank you."

He turned his head, his lips warm and soft as he pressed a kiss to her forehead. "Sleep, doll. I'll be here when you wake up."

* * *

Trent bolted upright in the bed and scanned the darkened room around him. His heart hammered like a freight train, and his chest was tight. He couldn't seem to catch his breath for the life of him. Images continued to pop through his mind, vivid and corporeal. The *boom* of the IED blast. The pain-filled screams of the team members who'd been out with him that day. Then total eerie silence before the blackness swallowed him.

Where the hell was he now? This wasn't the hospital. In the hospital, there'd been the steady beeps of the machines they'd hooked him up to. This appeared to be someone's house, but whose? His? Mom and Dad's?

He threw the covers back and swung his legs over the side of the bed when the light in the attached bathroom caught his attention. His mind filled with the image of Lauren, of the soft vulnerability in her eyes as he lay beside her on the bed, and reality rushed over him.

Lauren's. He was at Lauren's. In her bed.

"Fuck." He swore softly and released the breath pent up in his chest. Being in an unusual place had clearly triggered the nightmares. He'd never been in Lauren's bedroom before, and it had been too damn long since he'd slept beside another person.

He braced his elbows on his knees and ducked his head into his hands. His hair was damp, and his T-shirt stuck to his chest with the sweat he'd worked up in his sleep. The warm air blowing through the apartment cooled his overheated skin, sending goose bumps shivering up and down his bare arms.

How long he sat there he didn't know, but fatigue hung on him. The logical part of him told him to lie back down, but he couldn't make himself do it. The images wouldn't leave his mind. They swirled like buzzards around a dead carcass. He'd been here enough times to know. The instant he closed his eyes, they'd come again, and the thought had grief tightening like a steel band around his chest. Part of him didn't want to ever forget. Those men deserved someone to remember them.

A larger part of him simply wanted peace. He wanted to sleep a single night for a full eight hours. Wanted to wake up fully rested and not in a panic. So far since he'd come home, he hadn't been able to accomplish it even once.

The bed shifted behind him. "You okay?"

Lauren's sleep-roughened voice drifted through the darkness, calling to him like a lighthouse beacon, and the last of the tension finally drained from his body.

For her sake, he shot a smile over his shoulder, but couldn't bring himself to face her. "I'm fine. I'm sorry I woke you."

"It's okay. Was it the dreams again?"

He made a sound of acknowledgment, thought about feeding her a flimsy excuse. After all, he was supposed to be keeping his distance from her, and sleeping in her bed had him walking a fine, thin line. But neither could he resist her presence. He needed that special something about her that calmed the panic. "I woke up and couldn't remember where I was for a second."

He closed his eyes and swallowed hard. The memories continued to swirl, and the shaking wouldn't stop. More than he ever had, he longed to lose himself in her. To bury his face in her neck and inhale her scent. To find her mouth in the darkness and lose every thought in his head in the lush softness of her body beneath him.

"I'm okay. I just need a few minutes to reorient myself." If he touched her now, he didn't know if he could stop himself from doing everything he'd promised himself he wouldn't.

Lauren shifted in the bed behind him. It wasn't until her soft perfume floated around him that he realized she'd scooted up behind him. Her body warmed his back, but she kept her hands to herself. "Okay if I touch you?"

He wanted to laugh. It wasn't *just* okay. He needed that touch like he needed to draw his next breath. But he knew damn well he wasn't anything she needed or deserved, and right then his nerves were all on edge. He flat out didn't trust himself not to touch *her*. So he went for elusive and noncommittal. "I've passed the point where you need to tell me before you touch me. As long as you don't startle me, it's okay."

Lauren shifted again, setting her legs on either side of his, and wrapped her body against his back. Her arms came around his rib cage, her soft, warm hands resting on his pecs. She then laid her cheek against his back and went still. "I'm here if you need to talk."

The relief was so profound he couldn't stop the full-body shudder that moved through him. He let his shoulders slump as a sense of bliss enveloped him. He released a serrated breath, reached up to close his fingers around hers, and gave in to the pull of her. "I can't stop seeing him."

"Cooper?"

Her reply came softly, no judgment, simply honest curiosity. She was doing what she did best. She tended to pull shit out of him he shouldn't tell her. She didn't need to know this crap. The ugly stuff. And he hated the feeling he was somehow tainting her world by sharing it. But like always, her very presence soothed the wound itself, and damned if he could he resist.

He stroked his thumb over her knuckles, using her solidity to keep him grounded. He didn't have the words to tell her how grateful he was. "No. AJ. One of the guys I served with. He was only nineteen when he died. I have this image of his face, eyes frozen open in death. It was the last thing I saw before I passed out."

She didn't say anything for a moment, but a shiver ran through her, and he immediately regretted his harsh words.

"I'm sorry. I probably shouldn't tell you the gruesome stuff."

She stroked his chest, the action so damn soothing he gritted his teeth with the effort it took not to turn and wrap himself around her. "If you need to talk, Trent, I don't mind. I was actually thinking how awful it must be for you to have that image to remember him by. I'm guessing one of those tags you wear is his?"

So was the carved cross sitting in his bedroom closet.

"Yes." Vulnerability and grief moved over him. He closed his eyes, AJ's image floating into his mind. "He didn't have family, no one to mourn him. Didn't seem right. I wanted someone to remember him."

If at all possible, Lauren's hold on his chest tightened. "So you decided it should be you. That's very kind, but you have to forgive yourself. You're human. You can do both, you know. Remember AJ and forgive yourself."

He released a shuddering breath laden with too much regret. "That's just it. I don't think I can. He died because I screwed up."

"No. He died because the Taliban planted bombs intent on killing people." She leaned her head around his shoulder and took his chin in her hand, tilting his face to hers as much as their position would allow. "It's not your fault."

Whatever reply he had died on his tongue as her warm breath whispered over his lips. Inches, at most, separated them, and every breath she released teased his mouth, setting a fire bursting over his skin.

His train of thought skidded to a halt, then did an about-face. In two seconds flat he was hardening behind his fly, his heart once again hammering out an erratic staccato. More than he ever remembered, he ached to lean in and taste her. He couldn't forget kissing her. Couldn't forget the taste of her tongue or the softness of her lips or the quiet little whimper she'd let out.

It didn't help that her breaths were as jagged as his own. If he leaned in and kissed her now, would she let him?

She would and he knew it. *I realize that kiss probably meant nothing to you, but it was something to me.* She'd said that to him earlier. And he'd shot her down.

He sighed, the realization rolling over him. He owed her the truth. Not a mouthful of lies. "You were wrong, you know. When you said that kiss meant nothing to me. But right now I can't be anything you deserve. What I want at this point in my life is simple. I want to date for the first time in almost twelve years. I want to go out and have some fun, just because I can, and for the guys who don't have that luxury anymore. I want sex, doll, and a lot of it. But I have no desire to be tied down. Hell. I'm not even sure I'm capable of a relationship yet."

"Trent, I—"

"Let me finish." He swallowed hard and drew a breath for courage. If he didn't get the words out now, he'd never say them. "Don't think for one moment that I don't find you incredibly arousing. For the record, that kiss was phenomenal, and you set my world off its axis the night you propositioned me. I've thought of little else since. But I won't use you that way. I have far too much respect for you."

Then he waited, heart hammering in his ears. He wasn't sure he wanted to know what she thought.

Lauren moved first. She disentangled herself from him, lay back, and patted the bed beside her. "Come back to bed, Trent."

The light drifting in from the bathroom illuminated the room in a soft glow, allowing him to see her enough that she teased his senses. Her lean body and lithe curves. The longing in her gaze. Logic told him he needed to put some distance between them before he ended up hurting her. But the dreams and her selfless compassion had worn down his defenses. He didn't know what the hell happened now. He didn't want to think about it. But she offered comfort when he was attempting to shut her out, and he wasn't strong enough to resist her anymore.

So he crawled up the bed and slid over her, holding his weight on his elbows as he settled between her thighs. Her eyes widened in surprise, but her hands came to rest on his back and her knees bent to cradle his hips. Two layers of clothing separated them, but her soft, moist heat settled against the erection throbbing to life in his jeans. Trent ground his teeth, fighting the urge to rock into her, to slide his aching cock against her softness.

Fuck. He was going to lose his damn mind.

He bent his head, brushing his mouth over hers. Sipping. Tasting. Taking a privilege he damn well shouldn't, but one he couldn't resist either. Clearly he'd caught her by surprise, but she moaned low in her throat, and her mouth opened on a shuddering sigh. Her body melted beneath him, her hands sliding up his back to gather him closer. Yeah. He'd never in a million years get used to that. Or enough of it.

He allowed himself a taste. A moment to get lost in the suppleness of her lithe body beneath him. Her hot tongue swirling into his mouth and the quiet little whimpers and sighs emanating from the back of her throat. Then he forced himself to pull back, because he didn't think he could stop at a kiss.

He nipped at her bottom lip, then forced himself to slide off her. He lay on his back beside her, tried desperately to ignore the throbbing in his jeans—which were now too damn tight—and folded his hands over his stomach. If he didn't, he'd be rolling back.

Just his luck, Lauren snuggled up to his side and leaned her head against his shoulder. Every time he dragged in a breath, his lungs filled with the delicate mix of her fruity shampoo and the sweet musk of her perfume. "Thank you for being honest with me, but, Trent?"

He stared at her popcorn ceiling, watching the play of shadows. "Yeah?"

"I *want* you to use me."

His knuckles popped with the effort it took not to reach for her. Clearly he wouldn't be getting any more sleep. He'd be hard all fucking night.

CHAPTER SIX

Lauren woke the next morning to a vise squeezing her skull and a mouth that felt like someone had stuffed it full of cotton. The house around her lay still and quiet. Eerily so. No soft breaths in her ear, no solid body warming her side. Beside her the sheets were cold as well. Despite her senses telling her otherwise, she pried her eyes open and turned her head. As expected, the space next to her was empty.

She sighed into the room, trying her damnedest to stem the disappointment rising in her chest. After spending the night in his arms and that phenomenal kiss, waking to an empty bed and cold sheets left a hollow ache in her chest. Should she have expected anything more, though? Okay, so he'd admitted he was attracted to her, too, but his heart was still under lock and key. He'd told her as much. He'd also told her he intended to keep her firmly in the friend zone.

So why the disappointment this morning?

Because they'd shared a moment. It might have *only* been a moment, but her heart had clung to it. Telling her that their kiss had meant something to him, too, was like dangling a cookie in front of a woman on a diet.

She threw back the covers and pulled herself upright, groaning as the headache became a dull throbbing in her skull. A glance at the clock told her it was five minutes after nine. She'd hadn't slept this late in…years. She was usually up by three.

Never again. She was never drinking that much again. Another experience to check off her list, but something she wouldn't be repeating.

As for Trent, she *needed* to go back to the agency and set herself up with another date. Stop her heart from hanging on this one impossible dream. The trouble was, she had no desire to. Her heart had gotten stuck on a single man. Him.

Firmly shoving her thoughts aside, she pried herself out of bed and stumbled toward the kitchen, eyes half open. Halfway up the hallway, noise coming from the kitchen stopped her cold. The sound the glass coffeepot makes as it settles into the base.

Her heart skipped several giddy beats. There could be only one person in her kitchen this morning. Barely daring to believe it, she resumed her trek, but it wasn't until she came to a stop in the entrance that her mind finally accepted the fact. Trent. Not gone after all. He stood in front of the coffeemaker, wearing the same fitted jeans and long-sleeved shirt he'd had on last night. His hair stuck out at odd angles, but otherwise he looked the way he always did. Delicious.

She shook her head, unable to hide the awe the crept through her. "You're still here."

He peered over his shoulder and, at the sight of her, smiled. "Where else would I be?"

"You said you'd be there when I woke up."

Regret filled in his eyes, creasing his forehead.

"Sorry. After last night, I thought you could use some coffee and something in your stomach. Figured I'd wake you when it was done." He shrugged, adorably uncertain, then flashed a warm smile. "Breakfast should be ready in a few minutes."

Amazed by the sight of him, she stepped farther into the room, glancing around as she moved. Trent had the top of the coffeemaker open and scooped in grounds from a bag of locally roasted coffee. On the stove sat a nonstick skillet, and on the counter beside it, bread was doing its thing in the toaster. "What *is* for breakfast?"

Trent closed the coffeemaker and hit the brew button before moving back to the stove. "Eggs and toast. I always found something simple easier to stomach after a night of binge drinking. You like your eggs scrambled, right?"

"Yes." Color her impressed that he'd even remembered. Over the years, she'd stayed at his parents' house a lot, but being so much older, he was always gone. They'd rarely had breakfast together, save the few times he'd come home on leave.

She moved to stand beside him, watching for a moment as he cracked eggs into a bowl. One-handed even. Damn impressive.

She looked over at him. "Your mom teach you how to cook?"

Trent let out a quiet laugh. "Mom insisted we not get stuck in stereotypical roles. She insisted we all learn to take care of ourselves. Which meant Will and I had to learn to cook and do laundry, and Dad taught Mandy to fix her own car."

Drawn in by his warmth, Lauren couldn't resist a smile. A memory filled her mind. "Mandy told me that once. Said she enjoyed spending the time with your dad and learning that stuff."

He picked up a wire whisk and began to beat the eggs. "And I learned to like cooking."

"There's a certain soothing rhythm to it. Mom taught me. My adoptive mom, Mary, I mean. It's where I learned to love baking. She made the best cookies, and she made them for everything. Every holiday, every church social. Now, whenever I make a batch, it reminds me of her." She leaned sideways, bumping his shoulder. "Thanks for last night. For staying, I mean."

Trent shot her a warm smile. "That's what friends are for."

Those words from his mouth had the same effect as a glass of ice water dumped straight over her head. Whatever good mood he'd managed to build, he'd just sucked it right back out of her.

Lauren rolled her eyes, somehow resisting the urge to sock him, and turned instead to lean back against the opposite counter. She folded her arms. "Please. Say that one more time."

He darted a glance back at her, brow furrowed in confusion. "Say what?"

"Put me in my place. Next time I'm going to deck you. I really am. I get it, you know. I hear you loud and clear. Message received, sir." Eyes narrowed, she mock saluted him, then refolded her arms.

Trent studied her, those intense blue eyes searching her face for so damn long, unease pecked away at her. Well, she refused to run and hide this time. After discovering what his erection felt like pressed against her, to be reminded of her place in his life— again—was infuriating and confusing.

Seconds later, he seemed to make whatever decision he'd been pondering, for he pivoted and crossed the kitchen, coming to a halt in front of her.

"I thought I explained this last night, but maybe I need to

make it a bit more clear. Make no mistake about it." He thumbed her bottom lip, a tender stroke with all the warm familiarity of a lover. "I want you. Getting out of bed this morning was probably the hardest thing I've ever done, but I knew if I didn't, I'd have been seducing you out of those pajamas of yours. But I can't offer you forever, doll."

His thumb followed the line of her jaw, stroking her skin with such tenderness, she couldn't stop herself from leaning into his touch.

His pretty speech had also served to remind her why she had a crush on him in the first place. Deep down Trent was a good man. But she needed the answer to all the questions rolling around in her head. Good, bad, or ugly, she needed him to know where she stood. Clearly he had his own ideas, and he'd been brave enough to share them with her. She owed him the same in return.

She was going to have to get vulnerable with him again.

"For the record, I went on that date looking for a fling. I'm not sure Mr. Right exists, either. You want to know why I'm still a virgin at twenty-eight? Because I remember living with my birth mother. She went to work, kept the fridge full, but there never seemed to be any time for me. She was always getting ready for another date with another guy. Hell, she slept around so much she didn't even know who my father was. My adoptive mother, Mary, was the exact opposite. She was Roman Catholic and very involved in the church. She raised me to believe sex was sacred and should be between a husband and wife only."

Trent tucked his fingertips in his pockets. "Do you still believe that?"

Did she? "No. But it's why I waited. I didn't want to be anything like my birth mother."

He frowned, his intense gaze full of sympathy. "Your parents don't make you who you are, doll. You are who you choose to be."

She shrugged, turned her head, and idly stared at the stove clock as the memories of her childhood floated to mind. Going to church with Mary, learning the ins and outs of the religion. "Maybe, but it's what I feared for the longest time. I even made all these rules, for dating, for how I thought I should live my life. But they were just an excuse to keep people at a distance, to avoid getting hurt. It worked."

Vulnerability rose over her like a suffocating shroud. Lauren dropped her hand from his back and folded her arms instead. She had no idea if any of this even made sense to him, but she needed him to hear it, to know and understand.

"I went on that date determined to set myself free from all those rules, but last night made me realize something. I can deny it all I want, but I am who I am. I don't want a one-night stand with someone who won't remember my name the next morning.

"But I still want what I want. I still ache to know the tender touch of a man's hands. The intimate heat of his skin. I'm twenty-eight, Trent, and I have no idea what it's like to make love to someone. Or to be intimate with someone, period. So you can relax. I'm not trying to trap you. I just wanted to lose my virginity to someone I trusted, and I can't think of anyone who fits that bill better than you."

She pushed away from the counter and left the kitchen. In the living room, she stopped behind the couch, setting her hands along the top, and stared out the window. Ironically, it was a bright, beautiful day. Not a gray cloud in sight.

"But I can't just turn off my attraction to you because you want me to, either."

The sound of Trent's quiet footsteps moved up behind her, and she tensed, waiting. For what, she didn't know, but seconds later his body heat filled her back. He didn't, however, touch her. She couldn't be sure if that was good or bad, but her stomach knotted all the same.

His fingers stroked along her shoulder. Slow. Sensual. Careful. After a moment, he let out a heavy sigh. "And I'm no longer sure I want you to."

She let out a sardonic laugh. If she didn't, she'd lean back into him. Everything south of the border had turned hot and molten, and every nerve ending he touched flamed. "That's the most mixed-up thing I've ever heard, you know that?"

He looped his hands around her waist, setting his chin on his shoulder. "The last thing I want is to lose you."

"I didn't ask you to marry me. I believe I told you I just wanted to use your body for a while." She turned her head as much as their position would allow, looking at him out of the corner of her eye. Her insides wobbled, and nervous anxiety rolled through her stomach, but she had to take the chance or die a virgin. "If it's not going to be you, it's going to be somebody. If you don't want this, I understand, but at some point I'm going to have to move on. When I woke up this morning and found you gone, I had plans to call Military Match again."

His body stiffened against her back and his jaw tightened, nostrils flaring. "I can't stand the thought of your first time being with someone else, some asshole like last night."

"Then be my first." Lauren drew a deep breath and pressed herself into his arms, sliding her hands up his back. "It's not like I'm asking you to do me right here and now. It can happen at whatever pace you need it to."

He cupped her chin in his palm, brow furrowed, gaze intense. "You're okay with that?"

She lifted onto her toes, trying to close the space between them. "I'm okay with that. If it makes you feel better to put a label on this, consider us friends with benefits. When it stops being mutually satisfying, it ends."

She'd just have to be sure to keep her head in the right place, so that her heart didn't get broken in the end. This was a fling with a sexy guy, no more, no less.

He let out an agonized groan and brushed his mouth over hers, so lightly she shivered. "God, I can't resist you anymore. I have a few requests."

Her heart hammered in giddy anticipation. She hadn't expected him to accept. That he had sent myriad thoughts flying through her mind, all of which settled low in her belly. "Okay."

He pulled back. For a moment his gaze dropped as his fingers idly stroked her shoulder, like he couldn't help but touch her. "You can't tell Mandy."

Lauren rolled her eyes. "Trent, she's my best friend."

"Yeah, but she's *my* sister. The last thing I need is her privy to the intimate details of my prowess in the bedroom." He brushed his nose against hers, amusement glinting in his eyes. "I recall overhearing a conversation about *size* once."

Heat rushed into her face, but Lauren couldn't contain her grin. She recalled that exact conversation. They hadn't discussed him, exactly, but she remembered distinctly wondering.

"All right. On this I'll concede, because you have a point." She rubbed a circle over his chest. "What else?"

"I want to put a time limit on this. A month. When it's over, we go back to being just friends." His hands looped around her waist, pulling her flush against him. Heat flared in his eyes. "I also think we should ease into this. So my last request is no sex."

Lauren dropped her forehead to his shoulder with an exasperated sigh. "I'm never going to lose my virginity that way."

He chuckled and hooked two fingers beneath her chin, tilting her gaze back to his. His eyes blazed at her. "At least not right away. I'm proposing we do everything else first. Because I was thinking...you want the full experience, right?"

She shrugged. He had her there. "I guess."

"And that includes things like kissing. Touching." He leaned down, his voice lowering to a husky rumble against her mouth. "Tasting."

A hot little shudder moved through her as her mind filled with the possibilities: his rough hands closing around her breasts, fingers sliding into her panties, stroking her sex.

His warm mouth buried between her thighs.

"I like that idea. Doing it all. How 'bout, since you stayed last night, instead of lunch today, we start with dinner tomorrow night?" She pinned him with a direct stare and arched a brow, attempting to look fierce, but one corner of her mouth twitched, betraying her. "You still owe me a date."

He rolled his eyes but grinned. "Tomorrow's great."

"Then it's settled. You're mine starting tomorrow." She winked at him, then stepped back, took his hand, and headed for the kitchen. "Now, I believe you were making me breakfast."

CHAPTER SEVEN

Still on for dinner tonight?

Trent stared down at his cell phone, seated on the counter beside the stove. He was halfway through making breakfast when his phone buzzed in his pocket. The thought of seeing Lauren again had his heart sledgehammering his rib cage. Just reading her text made him so hard he ached.

He punched in a quick reply.

Yup. Can u b here by 6?

What they'd no doubt end up doing tonight filled his head, and if he didn't cool his jets, he'd need a cold shower before she even got here. Either that or he'd pounce on her the minute she stepped through the damn door. His body burned, and the only thing capable of dousing *this* flame was her.

His phone beeped and her reply popped onto his screen.

I can. What's for dinner?

That her reply arrived seconds after he'd sent his did nothing for the electricity fizzling along his nerve endings. It meant she was sitting somewhere doing the same thing he was—waiting on a text from him. Which filled his mind with visions of her. Was she in those pajamas he'd kill to peel off her? Or was she at work? He decided to ask.

Wait and see. ;) U at the shop?

Yes. Helping Elise fill all the custom orders. Anything I can bring tonight?

Nope. Just u. She was more than enough.

Great. C u later. I look forward 2 it, u know.

She had to go and say that. His cock twitched in his jeans, reminding him how long it had been since he'd last made love to a woman.

Me 2.

God help him when she got here.

* * *

By the time she actually arrived that night—five minutes early, no less—he was wound like a freaking top and so damn nervous he could barely stand himself. He'd spent the day reminding himself that he needed to take things slowly with her, for her sake, but one look at her as she stood on his doorstep had his brain scrambling. In a pair of jeans and a form-hugging, long-sleeved T-shirt, she looked good enough to eat, but those brown eyes filled with a heat and longing that burned him up from the inside out.

While some part of his brain said he ought to greet her, invite her in, Trent could only stare. Everything had changed between them. Their relationship had gone from platonic to sexual, and the quiet intimacy they'd shared last night flowed like an electric arc that leaped between them. Right then, he couldn't remember a single reason why he shouldn't pick her up and carry her back to his bed.

Focus, damn it! He wanted, needed, to do this right. According to their agreement, they'd make love for only one night, and he wanted her burning before that night arrived. She was a virgin, after all. He needed to take this one step at a time, not pounce on her like that jackass at her birthday party had.

He dragged a hand through his hair and stepped back, pulling the door open wider. "Come in."

Lauren stepped over the threshold, standing close enough her perfume floated around him, and opened the lid of a small black box she'd brought with her. Inside were six perfect dark chocolate truffles, the top dusted with a sprinkle of spice.

"I know you said I didn't need to bring anything, but I figured if you're cooking, I'd bring dessert." She plucked a chocolate from the box, holding it out to him. "Here, try one. These are new. I've started combining flavors. These are cardamom and chili."

Damned if his mouth didn't water at the sight. Since that first truffle she'd stuffed in his mouth that night nine months ago now, he'd become addicted to her chocolates. That was the night his attraction to her had started, and just like back then, taking this one from her meant eating it from her fingers. If he had to do that, he'd bust the damn zipper on his jeans.

When he didn't immediately take the bite, she wiggled it. "Come on. They're good. I promise. Try it."

Despite every instinct warning him against it, he leaned down, biting the chocolate in half. The familiar flavor melted on his tongue. The slight citrusy flavor of cardamom and a hint of spicy chilies filled his mouth, along with sweet, velvety dark chocolate. He closed his eyes, savoring the lusciousness melting on his tongue, unable to stop a quiet moan from leaving his mouth. "These are my favorites."

When he opened his eyes again, she studied him, keen interest mixing with a soft heat in her gaze. A pleased grin blossomed on her face, illuminating her eyes. "So you do eat my chocolate. I'm honored. I was sure after that first one I shoved in your mouth months ago you'd simply refuse to eat them."

He plucked the other half from her fingers, holding it to her lips. She hesitated, then opened her mouth and leaned forward, accepting the bite from him. "Exactly the opposite, actually."

The warmth of her mouth closing over his fingers had his heart skipping a beat. When her tongue actually brushed his index finger, his blood thickened, desire burning through him. When she closed her eyes and moaned, a soft little purr from the back of her throat, he fisted his hands to keep from bending down and tasting the chocolate on her lips. Oh, he hadn't counted on that.

He cleared his throat, forcing his brain to work, but the words left his mouth on a hoarse whisper. "I've bought a box every month since that first one. It's my guilty pleasure."

"Good." Lauren winked at him as she slipped her coat from her shoulders, then hung it on the rack by the door. As if to torment him further, she moved into the apartment, her fingers skimming his back as she passed him. The action set fire to every nerve ending she touched.

Halfway between the living room and the foyer, she stopped, sniffed the air, and peered back at him. Like she hadn't a clue that she had him dangling by a thread. "Smells good in here. What's for dinner?"

You.

He gave himself a mental shake and forced a smile. "You'll see. Come on. The rice should be about done."

He shoved his hands firmly in his pockets before leading her toward the living room. Halfway there, she wobbled on the stilts she was wearing and pitched sideways, catching his arm. He caught her around the waist, glancing at her shoes before looking over at her. "Why do you wear those things if you can't walk in them?"

A becoming pink flush rushed into her cheeks as she straightened, pushing off his shoulder. "Steph says they make my legs look longer."

He was married long enough to understand the hidden meaning in her shy statement. Namely, that she'd dressed for this date. So he did the only thing he could think of. He squatted at her feet, held out his hand, and peered up at her. "Give me your foot, please."

She furrowed her brow but did as he asked, and he slipped the shoe off and hurled it in the direction of the foyer. If he didn't get her out of these damn things, she'd either break her ankle or she'd be in his arms all night. He had plans for her, and they'd never get there if her soft body was plastered against his. He wanted to do this right, damn it. Not prove to her that he was just another selfish, clueless Neanderthal.

When her shoe hit the door with a loud *thunk*, the corners of her mouth tipped, amusement lighting in her eyes. "Hate my shoes that much?"

"No. I'd just rather you not break your ankle while you're here." He arched a brow and held out his hand. "Next foot, please."

He sent that one to its mate, then pushed to his feet and took her hand, tugging her behind him. As they entered the kitchen, he darted a sidelong glance at her. "For the record?"

"Yeah?"

"She's right. You look incredible in heels. I'd just rather you not hurt yourself." He released her hand and moved to the stove. Lauren remained silent, but her gaze seared into his back. He didn't dare look. If he did, he'd be doing everything he shouldn't. Right then his whole body burned. How the hell he'd get through tonight without pinning her beneath him was a complete mystery.

It didn't help that she stepped up beside him, her body brushing his arm. That musky perfume floated around him, teasing his senses, as she laid a hand on his back and leaned around his shoulder. "So, what's for dinner, tough guy?"

Firmly ignoring the heat of her body calling to him like a siren's song, he focused instead on the nickname. "Tough guy?"

She had the nerve to smile at him. Playful and, if he wasn't mistaken, flirty. "Yeah, for a SEAL, you're rather soft around the edges."

He couldn't help his grin. She was teasing him. The minx. Damn. She was in fine form tonight. Some logical part of his brain told him to let her comment go. Taking her up on the clear challenge in her eyes would do nothing but set their whole night off on the wrong foot. Slow. He was *supposed* to be taking this slow.

Once again, though, his mouth didn't appear to have gotten the memo. He arched a brow, tossing her grin right back at her. "There's nothing soft about me, doll."

She turned back to the pot on the stove and lifted the lid on the rice. "I'd like very much to see that for myself."

For a moment he could only stare and remember to drag in oxygen, because all his blood was currently seated in his jeans. Fuck. He couldn't remember the last time he'd been this damn aroused, and she hadn't even touched him.

Clearly she intended to kill him with sexual innuendos. When the hell had she learned to flirt like that?

"Rice pilaf." She picked up the wooden spoon resting on the stove and gave the rice a stir. Like she had no idea she had him by the cock. "Impressive. What else have you got planned?"

She looked over at him, blinking in expectation of an answer, but damned if he could make his tongue work. His mouth had gone dry.

He cleared his throat and turned back to the stove, lifting the lid on the skillet. "Crab cakes, and"—he moved back and pulled open the oven door—"roasted asparagus."

"I'm impressed. It smells divine and looks delicious." She turned toward him, a gleam in her eye, and swirled her index finger over his chest as she spoke. "You went all out."

He stifled a groan. Something was definitely different about her tonight, and if he didn't find out what—and soon—he'd bust the zipper on his jeans.

He folded his arms across his chest, because he didn't trust himself not to grab that finger and pull her in. "All right. I can't stand it. What's up with you? You're not yourself tonight."

He expected a playful retort. For her to toss something else provocative at him that would sever the last thread of his willpower. Instead, a soft pink flush stained her cheeks, flowing all the way up her neck.

Lauren rolled her eyes and pivoted away from him, leaning back against the counter. "I was *trying* to seduce you. Steph's idea. Apparently, it's not working."

He couldn't help the chuckle that escaped him. "That explains a lot."

"Don't. Laugh. You." She glared at him and jabbed a pointed finger at his chest, but the corners of her mouth twitched.

The last of his willpower went up in a puff of smoke. He turned toward her and pinned her back against the counter, cupped her ass in his hands, and lifted her off her feet, setting her down on the surface. Eye to eye now, he moved between her sleek thighs and leaned his hands on the counter on either side of her.

"I'm not laughing, doll, but if you don't stop teasing me, I'm going to plaster my mouth to yours, and I'm not sure I can stop there." He couldn't resist tracing her bottom lip with his thumb. Soft. She was so fucking soft, and he wanted to wrap himself up in her. "You have me so aroused right now I can't think straight. At least not about anything but burying myself inside you."

She slid her hands onto his waist and scooted closer, until her breasts grazed his chest and her heat settled against the bulge in his jeans. When he was taking every breath with her, she leaned forward and flicked her tongue along his lower lip. "So stop resisting."

He was going to have to get really honest with her. Any second now, she could decide she was done being patient with him and leave, and who the hell could blame her?

He sighed and set his forehead against hers. "It's been a while for me, doll, and my need is great. And you're a virgin. Chances are I'm going to hurt you just by default, and it scares the hell out of me. What if I can't be as gentle as you need me to be?"

Christ. That had to be the most honest he'd ever been with her. And it didn't make him feel strong to admit it, either. That he hadn't a freaking clue what he was doing. All he could do now was wait for the fallout of his confession. He was a Navy SEAL. He'd made it through BUD/S training and Hell Week. He'd been shot at by men intent on killing him. Hell, he'd been blown up. But not a single damn thing scared him more than she did.

She stroked a hand over his cheek, tender, warm, soothing. "I may not have experience in this department, but I don't believe that for one second. I don't want you to be anybody but you, Trent. And for the record, I happen to like you the way you are. A tough SEAL with a big soft heart. I don't think you give yourself enough credit."

Relief flooded his chest, and some of the tension knotting his shoulders finally eased. "Thank you. I just thought if we took it slow, did everything else first, by the time we get to the main course, you'll be so turned on, so wet, I'll just slide inside you, and it won't hurt so much. Because all you'll be thinking about is how much you want me."

"I appreciate that. And I'm okay with it." She brushed her mouth over his, a series of tiny kisses. "I'm told slow can be really good."

When he was crumbling at her feet, she pulled back, a wicked glint her eye, and braced her hands against his chest. She shoved him back, then hopped off the counter. Standing belly to belly with him, she once again held his gaze and his complete attention.

"Now, come on. You owe me dinner, and I don't know about you"—she tossed a saucy wink at him before turning back to the stove—"but I'm starved."

* * *

Heart hammering from somewhere around her tonsils, Lauren turned to the stove. Behind her, Trent had gone silent. His gaze, however, followed her every move, burning into her back, and it made her tremble. As she pulled the asparagus out of the oven, her hands shook so much the pan hit the edge of the stovetop in her clumsy attempt to set it down. Luckily, she managed to recover it in time to keep the damn thing from clattering to the floor.

She had no freaking clue what she was doing. After Trent left her apartment yesterday, she'd immediately called Steph. Steph had promised not to spill the beans to Mandy, for which she was grateful, then offered "pointers." Lauren had marched over here positive she could do this.

Until Trent plunked her ass on the counter and edged between her thighs. They'd officially reached the point where she was one hundred and ten percent out of her element. Her only plus right now was that he seemed to be responding to her awkward flirting. Who knew?

"Dinner can wait." Trent grabbed her hand and led her out of the kitchen. "I have something for you. I'd like to give it to you now, before I forget."

He led her down a long hallway toward the back of his apartment, then moved into his bedroom, stopping in the doorway of a walk-in closet on the right side of the room. "It's where I've hidden your birthday present."

Lauren couldn't help the soft gasp that left her. Instead of clothing hanging from racks, there were shelves lining the walls, each one holding hundreds of wooden carvings in a range of sizes.

She darted a glance at him. "You did all this?"

He released her hand and moved into the space. "It's a hobby.

It keeps the mind occupied. Well, most of the time." He shrugged.

She moved into the rectangular space, skimming her fingers along some of the smaller pieces lining the shelves. There were at least a dozen Santas, some that resembled trolls, more than a few dogs, and several garden gnomes. On the floor, carved from what must have been a tree stump, was a small black bear holding a three-tiered wedding cake. There was even a puppy hanging from a welcome sign. Trent had serious talent.

"Ever think about selling this stuff? I know all kinds of women who'd snatch this stuff up in a heartbeat. I could set up a counter in the bakery..." She moved to the cake-holding bear and touched his head, the possibilities rolling through her mind. "Set this guy up by the front door. Customers would go nuts for this stuff."

He stepped up to her side, staring down at the bear, the same way she was. "He's for you, by the way. The cake needs to be painted, but I thought I'd ask what colors you preferred before I did it."

Lauren jerked her gaze to his, unable to stop her mouth from dropping open. "You carved him...for *me*?"

He hitched a shoulder but didn't look at her. "A few of these pieces were inspired by you, actually. Like those gnomes over there? Mandy told me once you had a love affair with garden gnomes."

Lauren could only blink for a second. Not a single man in her life had ever done something so sweet before. She pivoted toward him and threw her arms around him. "This has to be one of the sweetest things anybody's ever done for me. Thank you."

He chuckled, his hands falling to rest on her waist. "I'm glad you like it."

"It's beautiful. I love it. That had to have taken you months to do." She pecked his stubbled cheek, then pulled back. She turned, intending to ask him about the puppy sign, when a large cross seated upright on an eye-level shelf caught her eye. It was tall and thin, much like the ones littering the war cemetery, but with an intricately carved design around the edges. She traced her fingertips over the name carved into the wood. "The young man who died."

Trent made a sound of acknowledgment as he came to stand beside her but didn't otherwise offer anything more. A glance at him found him staring at the cross with sightless eyes. No doubt lost in memories.

She laid a hand against his arm. "You should hang this on a wall."

He shrugged. "Don't know where to put it."

She studied him for a moment. He was stoic and withdrawn as always. Needing, somehow, to lighten the heaviness suddenly hanging over him, she carefully picked up the cross and turned it over to look at the back.

"Just needs a hook. You can get those in any craft store." She carefully tucked the cross under her left arm and took his hand, tugging him behind her as she made her way back into the living room.

He stood silent as she scanned the room. His furniture was sparse and practical, the space immaculately neat and clean. It honestly looked like it had been done up for an advertisement. The only human touch in the room were the pictures of his family on the mantel above the fireplace. She wanted to ask how he slept in this place, but she knew the answer. He didn't. At least not well.

"There." She tugged him around the couch and stopped in front of the fireplace. "On the wall. Or you could just set it on the mantel, I suppose, but it deserves a place of honor, because clearly he meant a lot to you."

When she looked over at him he was staring at her, blue eyes alight. He gave a slow shake of his head, a small smile tugging at the corners of his mouth, and turned. "Come on. Dinner's getting cold."

* * *

Lauren set the last glass into the top rack of the dishwasher and closed the door. Dinner had been…awkward. They'd made small talk, but tension had risen so high she'd expected something to shatter at any second. All the things they weren't saying to each other rose like a living, breathing entity. There was also an un-restrained hunger in Trent's gaze she'd never seen before, and it made her shiver.

Over the last twenty minutes, since they'd left the table, they'd cleaned the kitchen together, but the small talk had dwindled to only what was necessary to accomplish their task. Variations of "Hand me that plate? Thanks," and "You really don't have to do those."

It made her insides shake. She had no idea what the hell happened now.

She pushed the button to start the dishwasher, then leaned back against the counter beside Trent. "You've been very quiet."

He turned to her, his hands settling on her waist, and leaned into her. Whatever she'd been thinking deserted her. Trent was aroused. His erection was a thick bulge behind his zipper.

"Sorry. I'm nervous." He lifted a hand, his gaze following as he stroked his thumb along her lower lip. "I haven't done this in a while, and you're, well, you."

She let out a quiet laugh. "That makes us even then, because so am I." She lifted onto her toes, closing the gap between them, until her mouth hovered an inch from his. "Trent?"

"Hmm?" His gaze dropped, his voice taking on a distracted edge.

She flicked her tongue against his lower lip. "Shut up and kiss me."

Whatever had held him back up until this point seemed to fray. The same man who'd always been reserved and almost docile in her presence growled as he claimed her mouth. His hands shook as he cupped her ass and pulled her hard into him, rocking his erection into her soft belly.

Lauren couldn't stop a quiet moan from leaving her. God, it was only a kiss. It wasn't even their first. Instead of tender and coaxing, he was fierce and demanding. Heat flicked along every nerve ending, lighting that ember in her belly to a full-body burn. Shivers chased each other over the surface of her skin, leaving goose bumps, and everything south of the border became a hot liquid mass of need.

When she wound her arms around his neck and pushed back, rocking her hips into the intense connection, Trent leaned his forehead against hers, his fingers curling almost painfully into the flesh of her ass. His breaths blew harsh and ragged against her skin. "I don't know if I can be as gentle as you're going to need me to be. If I'm too rough, I need you to tell me. You've never been shy with me before. Please don't start now."

Was he really afraid he'd hurt her? She opened her mouth to reassure him, but he furrowed his brow, halting the words before they could leave her tongue.

"Promise me."

She rubbed the center of his chest, aiming for soothing. "I don't believe for one second that you'd hurt me or I wouldn't be here. Relax, Trent. I'm not worried. Neither should you be."

His breath left his mouth in a rush, his shoulders rounding as the tension left him.

She leaned in and pressed a soft kiss to his mouth, then slipped her hand into his and led him out of the kitchen. She stopped at the edge of the living room and turned to look at him. "Here or...the bedroom?"

Amusement glinted in his eyes. "We should probably stick with the living room for now."

She nodded and moved around the recliner that marked the beginning of the living room. The short walk to the sectional lining the far wall was the most nerve-racking one of her life. Trent followed in silence, but his gaze seared into her. By the time she came to a stop in front of his worn blue sofa, all the bravado she'd marched in there with deserted her.

She let out an uncomfortable laugh as she turned to him, flashing what had to look like a terrified smile. "I have to admit, now that I've dragged you in here, I haven't a clue what happens next."

One corner of his mouth quirked upward, and he hooked an arm around her waist, tugging her against him. "Well, it requires us to get a little closer."

The hunger in his eyes made her insides wobble, but the press of his warm, deliciously hard body against her had the butterfly party starting in her stomach. Her hands came to rest on his chest, but the only word she could manage to form was "Hi."

"Hi." He grinned and leaned down to brush his mouth over hers, then released her, took a seat on the couch, and crooked a finger at her.

Lauren swallowed the lump of rising fear, braced her hands on his shoulders, and climbed onto his lap, straddling his thighs. He sat for a moment, eyes heavy-lidded and filled with a heat that scorched her insides.

He slid his big, warm hands up her thighs to curl around her ass and tugged, pulling her tight against the hard bulge in his jeans, then caught her bottom lip between his teeth. "I need you. Too much."

Clearly he was more nervous than she was, the thought of which relaxed the tight ball in her stomach. At least she wasn't the only one with something at stake here.

She stroked her fingertips through the short hairs at his nape. "Tell me something. Do you like it rough?"

"Yes and no." He shrugged, but heat flared in his eyes. "Sometimes a good hard fuck is exactly what you need. Wild and unrestrained."

She had no idea if he meant his words as the tease they were, but a hot little shiver raked the length of her spine, settling in her damp panties. The meaning behind the words, however, told her a lot. "And you can't do that with me."

Trent cupped her cheeks in his hands, thumbs sweeping her skin. "Not yet."

She leaned in, pressed her breasts against his chest, and brushed her mouth over his. "Trent?"

His gaze locked on hers, eyes blazing. "Hmm?"

"For the record…that thought turns me on more than a little. You pinning my hands above my head so I can't move and shoving so hard into me the headboard knocks the wall."

She closed her eyes as the image slid over her. She could almost hear the huff of his breathing in her ear, the slap of flesh on flesh. Her insides clenched in luscious anticipation and, unable to help herself, she rolled her hips, grinding against the bulge behind his zipper. Pleasure erupted from the point of contact, seeping over her nerve endings, and a quiet, needy moan escaped.

"God, that's the stuff of fantasies." She forced herself to pull back, because she needed him to know, to understand. "It's important to me that you enjoy this, too. I don't *want* you to hold back. If you get nothing out of this, then I don't either."

He let out a low, husky laugh and nipped at her bottom lip. "Oh, believe me, doll. I'm going to enjoy the hell out of you."

Lauren rolled her hips again, grinding against him, and bent her head, scraping her teeth over the fleshy muscle of his shoulder. "Trent?"

A shudder moved through him, and his fingers tightened on her ass. When she pulled back, he had his eyes closed, mouth hanging open in awe. "Yeah?"

She leaned her mouth to his ear. "Then shut up and fuck me."

CHAPTER EIGHT

Trent bit back a groan. God, she had to go and say that. He couldn't remember ever wanting a woman as much he did her. He was shaking, for crying out loud. Having given himself permission to want her, taking steps to actually *be* with her was like opening the floodgates. What he really wanted was to rip her clothes off, to feel all that warm, supple skin against his.

But that meant taking *his* shirt off, and the thought made his insides shake. Outside of the doctors and nurses, nobody had seen the scars dotting his torso, healed wounds from the shrapnel they'd taken out of his skin. His right arm contained the scarred-over remains of the burns he'd suffered when the IED detonated. It wasn't pretty. Would it bother her?

Oh, they'd have to get there sooner or later. He just wasn't ready to do it now. He'd *hoped* they could take things slowly. One step at a time. So that when they actually made love, they'd be more comfortable with each other and it wouldn't matter.

Lauren let out a nervous laugh and dropped her gaze, smoothing a hand over his chest. "I'm sorry. That was really out there.

I got caught up in the moment. Steph told me once men like it when you talk dirty."

Great. Here he was, too caught up in his own damn thoughts. *Pull your shit together, man.*

He smoothed his hands up her back, gathering her closer. "I'm sorry about my reaction. You just surprised me. I've never heard you talk like that before."

Her mouth now inches from his, Lauren traced a fingertip along his bottom lip. "Is that good or bad?"

He skimmed his hands up her thighs and over the curves of her ass, tugging her the tiniest bit closer, so that she could feel for herself what her words had done to him.

"It's good. Steph's right. It's a huge turn-on, especially coming from you." She shivered, her eyes falling closed, and he bent his head, trailing his lips along the cord of muscle where her neck met her shoulder. "Tell me something. Is that what you want? To fuck?"

A soft, serrated breath left her, and her fingers curled, nails scraping his skin as she fisted his shirt in her hands. "I honestly don't know. You said you wanted to go slow. I liked the idea, but…"

The hesitation in her voice stopped him. He lifted his head and stroked his thumb along her cheek. "But what? Be honest with me."

Her eyes opened, heavy-lidded, full of a desire that still filled with him awe to see. "But I'm really out of my element with all of this. I don't know where to start or where to touch you."

He was every bit as lost as she was when what she really needed was someone to take charge. Firm in the thought, he pulled up the Navy SEAL. The side of him that knew what to do and wasn't afraid to take charge. Then he slid his hands up her stomach, skimming the undersides of her breasts.

"For what it's worth, I thought we'd start with kissing and then take it from there. Keep the clothing on. For now at least." He arched a brow, aiming for playful. "That okay with you?"

She blinked at him. "A first step."

"Exactly. As for where to touch me, that's completely up to you. You told me recently you think about me when you're alone at night. What do you imagine?"

Lauren rolled her eyes, the flush in her cheeks deepening. "I told you that because I was angry with you."

He couldn't help his grin. She hadn't a damn clue telling him that was a fantasy he'd pondered a lot over the last nine months.

"I like the thought of you touching yourself while thinking of me. I think about you, too." He leaned in, catching her bottom lip between his teeth. "Now answer the question."

She drew a shaky breath, her gaze flicking to his, hot as hell itself. "Think about me how?"

He swallowed a groan. He was going to come in his jeans before this night was over. That question right there, along with the hooded desire in those gorgeous eyes, only served to add fuel to the flame raging through his blood.

"This. All of it. Your warm, soft skin against mine. The taste of your breath. What part of your body's the most sensitive." He skimmed his hands up her thighs again, letting his thumbs graze her heat. "I often find myself with my cock in my hand, wondering what sounds you make when you come."

A full-body shudder moved through her, a quiet, shaky breath leaving her. "God, that's so damn sexy."

His fingers flexed against her thighs with the frustration winding through him, with the effort it took not to touch. He drew a breath and forced his fingers to relax. "Answer the question, doll. How?"

This time she held his gaze, bold as brass. "I think about you at night, when I'm lying in bed and I can't sleep. Thought about you just last week, actually. And my hands wandered into my panties." She glanced down, fingers skimming the hairs on his arms. "I like to imagine your hands. I don't have any reference for sex, or what it should feel like, but you have fantastic hands. I like to imagine that it's your fingers touching me instead of my own."

A deep groan finally made its way out. He dropped his head back against the sofa, unable to resist sliding his hands to her ass and tugging her the slightest bit closer. Until he was sure he could feel the moist heat of her against him. "You're killing me here, you know."

Her hands stopped moving then, coming to rest over his pecs and burning his skin through his shirt. Those eyes filled with mischief, one corner of her mouth quirking upward as she leaned into him, pressing her breasts into his chest. Her nipples were hard as diamonds, and her warm breaths whispered over his mouth. "You did ask."

He rolled his eyes and parroted her earlier words. "So I did. Now shut up and kiss me."

He meant the words as a tease, but her soft smile faded. She studied him for a moment, gaze working his face. That sweet, fiery tension filled the air around them, until he was dragging in labored breaths, his heart hammering an erratic beat.

She leaned in, brushing a timid kiss across his mouth. He let his hands wander up her back, smoothing slowly over her as he luxuriated in the simple ability to touch her, to feel her body. He was content to let her take her time and kissed her back the same way, a tangle of lips, a flick of his tongue.

Whatever nervousness they'd begun with slowly evaporated. She let out a soft moan and tilted her head, her soft lips slanting over his. Her mouth opened, and damned if he could resist flicking his tongue out to taste her. When she reached back, a needy groan ripped out of him. He gripped her head in his hands and pulled her to him. Shaking now with an unquenchable thirst, he spent long minutes drinking her in, drowning in the hot, heady wetness of her mouth.

Lauren gave as good as she got. Her fingers slid into his hair and curled against his scalp, the pressure of her lips against his almost brutal and desperate. Soft mewling noises emanated from the back of her throat, hungry sounds that only increased the ache in his jeans.

All the while she rocked into the pulse of his erection. Her breathing grew rapid and shallow, becoming an erratic huff in between sips and tastes. Every brush of her heat against him shot pleasure to his fucking toes. He needed to slow down. Like hell would he come in his jeans, as if he were some inexperienced kid.

Nor could he force himself to stop her. The quiet mewling became a series of desperate moans that filled his soul. He *needed* her pleasure. So he skimmed his mouth along her shoulder. Licking. Sucking. Scraping his teeth lightly over the skin exposed by the scoop neckline of her top. He dragged his fingertips up her sides and curled his palms around her breasts. She was a delicious little handful, and her nipples strained against the confines of her bra. He couldn't resist flicking his thumbs across the tightened tips. She rewarded him with another needy moan and pressed closer, pushing her breasts into his hands.

Her every reaction made his chest swell in triumph. He was the first man to ever touch her this way, which made her feel a little too much like his. Every soft shiver fueled the need burning through him to make this good for her. He wanted her to leave their time together glad she'd experienced it. He wanted to fulfill every single one of her fantasies in a way that was starting to scare the hell out of him.

When she began to tremble in his arms, her thighs shaking on either side of his hips, experience told him her orgasm was close. He turned his head and nuzzled her earlobe. "Let it go, Lauren. Come for me, doll."

Hands braced on his chest, she shivered and pressed closer. It was almost painful how good it felt. Two layers of thick denim separated them, but he swore he could feel her moist heat sliding along his length as she ground herself against him.

He *tried* to focus on her, kissing and stroking every part of her he could reach. But every time she rocked into him, his erection strained against his jeans and pleasure erupted over his skin. He hadn't been with a woman in almost two years, and two years of need built on top of his yearning for *her*.

So he gave in and simply buried his face in her neck. The musk of her perfume filled his nostrils every time he inhaled. Hands on her ass, he pulled her to him, thrusting against her in time with her own, reveling in the almost unbearable pleasure shooting along his nerve endings every time she ground against him.

"Trent…" That was all the warning he got. With a soft gasp, Lauren dropped her head back and began to shake quietly in his arms. The fluid rocking of her hips became an erratic jerking as her orgasm took over.

Trent froze, awed by the sight above him: her brow furrowed

in sweet agony, her soft mouth hanging open in bliss. She didn't make a sound. He wasn't even sure she breathed, but holy God damn it had to be the most beautiful sight he'd ever seen.

By the time she collapsed against him, *he* was spent and exhausted, and he hadn't even come.

Lauren panted into his neck, her body limp in his arms. "That was incredible."

Shaking right along with her, he wrapped his arms around her back, crushing her to him, and kissed her shoulder. "*You're* incredible."

They sat for some time in companionable silence. He was content to simply hold her, stroking her back.

When her trembling lessened and her breathing returned to normal, she finally stirred against his throat. She tilted her head and kissed his neck, then wound her arms around his back. "Can I ask you something? It's kind of a stupid question."

He let his fingers follow the delicate curve of her spine. "There are no stupid questions."

"I wanted to ask if it was good for you, but then it occurred to me. You didn't come with me, did you?"

"No." Not that he was sorry for it. If he died tomorrow, he'd die a happy man. He'd gotten to watch her come undone and know *he'd* been the one to put that bliss on her face. It made him want to beat his chest like a freakin' ape. He was shaking with the overwhelming desire to make her do it again as many times as he could before her body simply gave out. "I make a bigger mess than you do. Besides, it wasn't about me just then."

She lifted her head, brow furrowed, eyes pinning him to his spot. "This is supposed to be mutual. It doesn't work for me if you get nothing out of this."

He bit back a laugh. She really had no idea. "Believe me, doll, I got plenty out of that. You're damn beautiful when you let yourself go."

She studied him for a moment. Decision apparently made, she reached for the button on his jeans, popping it free, and slipped her hand into his pants. Her supple fingers slid along his cock and curled around his length, her palm warm and soft as it ghosted over his flesh.

"Fuck." He closed his eyes, dropped his head back against the sofa, and gave himself over to her. He hadn't been touched by anything other than his own damn hand in almost two years, and her fingers were the closest to heaven he was sure he'd ever get.

When he stopped resisting, she curled her hand more firmly around him. Very quickly, she gained a rhythm, her hand moving at a speed that flat-out amazed and awed him. Every stroke sent heat prickling along the surface of his skin and pleasure spreading like wildfire.

In less than a minute, she had him on the desperate edge of release.

She leaned her mouth to his ear, her fingers changing angle and speed but never stopping. "Is this okay? Am I doing this right?"

The uncertainty in her voice caught him. He needed to tell her she was doing more than okay. She fucking amazed him. Not that he could find the right words or make his tongue work enough to say them. So he reached out blindly, managed to find her thigh, and squeezed.

As if somehow she understood, she released a pent-up breath. Then she leaned in and nipped at his earlobe, laving the small wound with a stroke of her tongue. "Let go. You want to know what I think about at night? This. Getting to watch your pleasure. That turns me on, too."

The husky rumble of her voice in his ear lit him up like a Fourth of July firework. He came with a hoarse groan, his orgasm ripping through him, blinding and hot. His hips jerked into her hand, his come splashing his shirt. When the spasms finally ended, he collapsed back into the sofa.

Bone-weary and feeling too much like a limp noodle, he sat there for a minute in stunned silence, attempting to make his lungs works again. Contrary to the take-charge woman who'd ripped his jeans open, Lauren laid her head on his shoulder, snuggling into his neck. Her fingers continued to stroke him, softer and slower now, but sending small sparks shooting along sensitive nerve endings.

He let out a tired laugh. "You really are going to wear me out."

She laughed, too, and turned her head, kissing his throat.

When he caught himself drifting off, he opened his eyes and kissed her forehead. "I need to get up, doll. I'm fairly certain I just made a mess out of both of us. That's your fault, by the way."

She pulled her hand from his pants. "Do I sound like I'm complaining?"

She got up all the same, sliding off his lap to stand in front of him. He tucked himself back in his jeans but didn't bother doing them up, because he had to change them anyway, and grabbed her clean hand. "Come on. I'll get you a fresh shirt."

She followed quietly behind as he led her down the hall into his bedroom. Once there, he released her hand and moved to his dresser, retrieving a clean T-shirt for each of them, a new pair of jeans for himself, and returned to her.

"You're incredible, by the way." He pressed a soft kiss to her lips and attempted to turn away, but she grabbed a fistful of his shirt and pulled him back.

"Ditto." Her eyes gleamed as she kissed him again.

Then she took a T-shirt from his hand, shoved him out the bedroom door and closed it in his face. He couldn't stop a goofy-ass grin from blooming, but turned and headed for the bathroom.

Ten minutes and one quick cleanup later, he emerged from the hallway into the living room. Lauren sat once again on the sofa. She had one leg tucked up against her belly, the other curled beneath her, staring with sightless eyes at the dark television screen on the opposite wall. As he stepped into the room, she turned to look at him. Something vulnerable and tender flashed in her eyes, catching him in the chest.

Yeah. There it was. The moment when the desperate desire to come together hard faded, leaving two people who'd been intimate only minutes ago feeling like strangers. With her, it just felt wrong. It created a wall between them, and every cell in his body rebelled against the idea. The problem was, he had to let that feeling remain there. It neatly severed any ties they might have formed tonight.

And they had formed them.

Being with her was so damn easy. She fit. Like his favorite pair of boots, or those jeans he'd had for going on five years now. They were worn and soft and familiar, and they fit like a glove. Being intimate with her only seemed a natural next step.

She made him want. For the first time since he'd come home, since the divorce, the need for more swelled in his chest. Because somehow, when he was with her, she filled all those holes he'd come home with.

Lauren smiled, polite but awkward, and he was moving to her before he'd decided what the hell to do now. He took a seat on the sofa, hooked an arm around her shoulders, and gathered her to him. She slid an arm over his belly, and he tucked her securely against his side and rested his cheek on top of her head.

They sat that way for a while, the air filling with all those things they weren't talking about. Finally, he couldn't stand it.

"I'd like to ask to you to stay, but I don't trust myself. I'm not sure I'd be able to resist you." He wanted her too damn much. If she lay in bed beside him, those lean curves against him all night, what on earth would stop them from making love? Except his conscience. One taste of her would never be enough.

She remained silent for a moment. Then her fingers grew restless, stroking over his belly. "I know. Because we're not making love yet."

He hated the thought of sending her home, but he needed the illusion of distance with her all the same. When this month ended, she'd go back to being a friend. He needed her to. By allowing himself this time with her, he was already breaking his own rule—to never get involved with her. No, it was better for the both of them if he separated himself from this now.

She'd already seen too much of what he went through at night. The nightmares and sleeplessness. He refused to taint her world with that crap any more than he already had.

Neither could he let her go yet. "We could watch a movie."

Her head rocked against his shoulder. "Sounds good."

He reached for the remote on a side table. "Let's see what's on, then."

Two hours later, they stood by the front door. The movie hadn't done him any damn good. It just meant he had two hours to hold her. Two hours to ponder how big of an ass he was for sending her home in the first place. Two hours to think of all the things he ought to be doing instead. Like carrying her back to his bed and curling around her. And making her breakfast in the morning.

If she noticed his anxiety, she didn't say anything. Rather, she slipped her hands around his rib cage and up his back, pressing her soft body into his. Back in her heels now, she nearly matched him in height, so that she merely had to lean in to touch her mouth to his.

Her brows rose, the question in her eyes even before the words left her mouth. "So, how 'bout we meet on the weekends? I figure we both have to work early on weekdays, and I don't know about you, but by the time I get home from work, I'm pretty much worthless."

He thumbed her chin and pressed another soft kiss to her lips. "Weekends are perfect."

"Good. See you next weekend, then." She winked at him, then moved out the door, closing it softly behind her.

For a moment he could only stand and stare at the space where she'd been. If sending her home was the best thing for her, then why did he feel like such an ass? Like he'd just become the one thing he swore he wouldn't—just another jerk on her list. Didn't that make him little better than the asshole he'd chased from her party last night?

He shouldn't be with her at all…

CHAPTER NINE

Lauren shoved the till closed and offered the customer across from her a friendly smile. "See you tomorrow, Gayle."

A businesswoman in her midforties, Gayle pursed her mouth, frowning down into the white bag. "You're ruining my diet, you know, with these scones of yours. I pass this shop every day on my way home and every day I can't resist stopping in."

Lauren laughed and winked. "I'd say I was sorry, but…"

Gayle laughed and winked back. "Me too." She lifted a hand in farewell, then turned, calling out as she made her way to the exit, "Here's hoping I'm stronger tomorrow."

As she watched Gayle exit, the familiar rumble of an engine sounded seconds before a gleaming black motorcycle glided to a stop in front of the store. The black beast was gorgeous. The rider seated on it had her heart skipping a beat. Trent. He pulled off his helmet and hung it on the handlebars before pocketing his keys and getting off the bike. He stopped on the front walk, caught her gaze through the glass, and grinned.

Her heart skipped several more beats as she watched him pull open the front door and stride, casual-like, to the register where she stood. They'd texted back and forth every day, but three days had passed since she'd actually seen him. In worn jeans and that soft black leather jacket, he looked more delicious than the cupcakes they'd made this morning.

He leaned his elbows on the glass countertop and peered up at her. "Hey."

"You look like you're in a good mood." She hadn't seen him this relaxed in all the time he'd been home. It was a good look on him.

If at all possible, his smile widened. "Been a good day. We finished a gorgeous bike and the customer loved it. Thought I'd stop by on my way home to see what time you get off."

She was tempted to tease him and tell him it depended entirely on him, but bit her tongue. They weren't alone. Elise was in the back cleaning up the morning dishes. "About six. Why?"

"Thought so. Wanted to stop by the apartment and bring your birthday present down. I'll need to go borrow Will's Beamer first, but I thought maybe afterward you might like to have dinner with me." He reached across the counter and took her hand, stroking his thumb across her knuckles. "I know we agreed on weekends, but I couldn't resist seeing you. Take a ride with me later?"

So he'd spent the day thinking the same thing she had—dreaming up reasons to come see her. The thought made her tingle all over. Neither could she resist.

"It's ironic you're here, actually. I planned to come see *you* tonight. I'll tell you what." She lowered her gaze to their hands and turned his palm over, twirling her index finger in aimless circles over the center. "I'll have dinner with you if you bring me a few of those pieces in your closet, too. I cleared some shelf space for you this morning, over by the door."

She nodded, indicating the shelf across the room. The idea had formed as she'd stood in his closet, looking at them all, but when she'd walked into the shop this morning, a certain shelf by the door had caught her attention. Trent had talent. His beautiful pieces needed to be seen.

The light left Trent's eyes, and he pulled his hand back and straightened. "You really think anybody will pay money for those?"

She didn't have to ask to know why he was tense. His reaction when he'd shown her his closet had told her in no uncertain terms his carvings were private, the workings of his imagination in a painful moment. But she wanted him to know, to believe, that his carvings weren't as ugly as the memories that had inspired some of them.

She moved around the counter and laid a hand against his chest. "Trust me?"

Frown lines formed around his mouth, those blue eyes working her face. "You really want to do this."

"Not if you really don't want me to, but…you have them hidden away like they're something dark and hideous when I think they should be put out on display. You took something painful and turned it into something truly beautiful. You should be proud of them." Hoping somehow to sooth the wound she'd clearly just poured salt into, she shrugged and shot him a playful grin. "If they don't sell, you can tell me I told you so, and I'll keep them for decoration. Because *I* love them."

Finally, he rolled his eyes, the stiffness leaving his shoulders. "Fine. Six pieces."

She rubbed her hand over his chest, serious now. "Give me your favorites. The ones you're the most proud of."

His gaze narrowed, and he leaned down, touching his nose to hers. "You drive a hard bargain, Miss Hayes." He kissed her cheek and pivoted, waving a hand behind him as he strode for the front entrance. "See you in an hour."

Exactly an hour later, Trent pulled up out front, not in Will's silver BMW, but in Skylar's red Mercedes. Lauren watched through the front windows as he climbed from the SUV, moved around to the rear, and popped the hatch. He pulled out a dolly cart and set it on the ground, then hefted out the carved bear. This was one of those days when she sincerely wished it was warmer. She was sure under the bulk of his leather jacket, those biceps of his were bulging, and God how she would have loved to watch.

Elise came to stand beside her, resting her hands on the glass surface, and nodded in Trent's direction. "What's he got?"

Lauren answered without looking. "My birthday present. He carved that. Can you believe it? I'm having him set it up by the front door. An impromptu welcome sign if you will. I think it's adorable."

Trent came through the front door then, pushing it open with his behind as he wheeled the dolly in.

Elise gave a hum of appreciation beside her. "Nice backside, that one."

Lauren jerked her gaze to her friend, who'd never once in the five years she'd been working here made such a blatant remark. "Elise!"

Elise gave a lighthearted laugh and winked at her. "I'm old, sweetie. Not dead."

Elise turned her gaze out front again. They stood for a moment, watching Trent heft that not-small bear into the corner by the front window. When he had it in place, Elise let out a low whistle, then turned and headed to the back room, leaving Lauren giggling in her wake.

Lauren rounded the counter, moving toward Trent as he adjusted the bear to face the window. "You better have brought the others with you or you'll be having dinner on your own this evening."

"Slave driver." Trent chuckled. Bear in place, he straightened and closed the space between them, standing this side of too close. His scent swirled around her, fresh air and something uniquely him. His eyes narrowed, glinting with a heady mixture of amusement and heat. "I have ways of convincing of you to have dinner with me, you know."

Never one to back down from a fight, playful or otherwise, Lauren straightened her shoulders and took a step toward him, until her belly brushed his. Not that she could resist the urge to tease him. The play between them was addicting. He was sexy as hell when that mischievous gleam lit in his eyes. "Is that a threat or a promise?"

He darted a glance behind her, then hooked an arm around her waist and dragged her flush against him. "Oh, that's a promise, doll."

Lauren's breath caught, and for a moment she could only stare at him. Oh, she hadn't expected him to do that. Trent was mightily aroused.

He leaned down, turning his mouth to her ear. "I've been hard for three days thinking about you." Just as quickly, he pulled away and pivoted, leaving her to stare after him as he headed for the front entrance. "Come on. You can help me bring the carvings in."

Ten minutes later they stood staring at the shelf where she'd set the carvings up on display. Turned out a few of the pieces he'd brought over were the ones he'd told her he'd carved for her—a set of three female garden gnomes. One of them was a dark-haired baker holding a cupcake and wearing an apron, another, an older female with a basket of flowers, and finally, there was a cute little gentleman asleep leaning against a mushroom.

He'd also brought an old-fashioned Santa, which she knew his mother collected, and two dogs, a beautiful German shepherd, and a Labrador retriever. Tomorrow she'd make him a sign, letting the public know they were carved by a local artist.

Trent's hand slid into hers where it rested at her side, his long fingers threading through hers. "I appreciate your faith in me, you know."

She squeezed his fingers and looked over at him. "So where are we headed?"

Not that she cared. She only had a month with him like this. She intended to enjoy the time she had. Letting him go would be hard. She'd have to let him put her back in that safe little box he seemed to keep her in. It would be worth it, though, because for a month he was hers.

He finally glanced over at her, blue eyes relaxed and searching her face. "I have to give Skylar back her car and pick up my bike first, but I thought we'd take a ride to the waterfront. We could stop somewhere along the way and get some takeout, bring it to Chism Park?"

She smiled and nodded. "Sounds good."

An hour later they stood staring out over the waters of Lake Washington. Dinner had been Chinese. They'd sat in the grass, eating from paper cartons, and talked about their days while staring out over the serene lake. Trent stood behind her now, his arms wrapped around her waist, his chin resting on her right shoulder.

They'd been standing there for some time, holding each other, a comfortable silence between them. Trent, however, hadn't quite relaxed. His body was tense and his hands continually moved, skimming along her waist, fingers dipping beneath the hem of her shirt to stroke her skin. More than once he'd kissed her neck, her shoulder, brushed her earlobe with his nose.

That was as far as he'd taken it though. Clearly he wanted more as much as she did.

She stroked her hands along his arms, the leather of his jacket soft beneath her fingers. "Can I ask you something?"

"Sure."

"Why are we here? I assumed when you showed up at the shop that we'd…" She shook her head, letting the words flit away on the soft breeze. God, it seemed so stupid now.

He turned his head, skimming his lips along the side of her neck. "Thought maybe if we came out here, you wouldn't be so tempting."

The husky rumble of his voice against her skin lit a blaze in the pit of her stomach. "May I ask why?"

"Because we're supposed to be taking it slow." He released a heavy sigh and rested his chin on her shoulder again. "I know we both have to work early in the morning, but I couldn't resist. I had to see you."

She slid her hand along his arm, threading her fingers with his. "We can do everything but, correct?"

"That's the idea, yes."

She twisted at the waist to peer over her shoulder at him. "Then take me home."

Hunger flared in his eyes, and he let out a groan, this one tormented and filled with need. "You know, the fact that I can't resist you is going to get me into trouble one day soon."

He brushed his mouth over hers, then took her hand and pivoted, leading her back to where he'd parked his bike in the lot.

She had to hand it to him. He drove carefully, going the speed limit and concentrating on the road. She wasn't sure she'd have been quite so calm. At least he was until they reached her place. The door barely closed behind them before he pressed her back against the foyer wall. His mouth came down hard on hers, his kiss restless and urgent. His hands went everywhere. Stroking up her sides and skimming her breasts, then sliding back down to cup her ass and pull her hard against him. If at all possible, his erection was thicker and harder than it had been at the park.

When he finally pulled away, he was breathing as hard as she was. He caught her gaze for a split second, then took her hand and led her to the bedroom at the back of the house. Once there, he climbed onto the bed and pulled her down with him.

Draped over his chest now, hands caught between them, Lauren peered at him. He let out a deep groan, his hands sliding down to cup her ass, holding her to him for a moment. Then he lifted his head, kissing her softly.

"Same rules as last time." He narrowed his eyes, though one corner of his mouth hitched, contradicting the fierceness of the look. "That means no touching, you."

She might have laughed, but his words caught her, and she shook her head, brow furrowing with her frustration. "That means you don't get anything out of this. I'm not okay with that."

The memory filled her mind of the last time they were together, and a full-body shudder moved through her. Her breath left her mouth on a shaky exhalation, her core throbbing.

She leaned down, murmuring against his lips, "God, that was incredible. Getting to see your pleasure."

Hunger filled his eyes. He lifted his head, skimming his lips along the skin exposed by the neckline of her top. "That's an idea, you know, as an alternative."

She didn't have to ask to understand what he meant. The image—a longtime fantasy—filled her mind, and a heated shiver moved through her. Fire licked along every last nerve ending, and perspiration broke out along her skin, the room suddenly sweltering. A quiet moan escaped. God, if she wasn't wet already at the thought.

"Yes." She nipped at his bottom lip.

Laughter rumbled out of him. "What, no protest?"

She shook her head. "You have no idea."

"For me, too." He nipped at her bottom lip, then lifted her and rolled her over, holding himself up on his elbows. "The rules will have to change a bit. I'd imagine it won't be very comfortable for you in those jeans, and there's no way for me to stroke myself without you getting an eyeful."

She squirmed beneath him and waggled her brows at him. "I'm okay with that."

He closed his eyes and dropped his forehead to her shoulder. "You're killing me here, you know."

"I'm sorry. I'm just teasing. I'm nervous. I've never..." She shook her head, letting the words trail off into the silence. Heat rose up her neck, flooding her face. Here she was, admitting she was a naive virgin. Surely that had to be the biggest turnoff ever.

He lifted his head, brushing a tender kiss across her mouth. "Me either."

"You and Wendy never?"

"No. Wasn't her thing." He shrugged and kissed her again, this one softer, slower, eventually melting into a luscious tangle of lips and tongues. Her hands slid up his back, as if to somehow gather him closer, fire rushing over her skin.

Time seemed to pass in eons. There was only him, simply the luscious scent of him and the heady flavor of his mouth and the delicious weight of him pressing her into the mattress. If there was a heaven, it was here in his arms. God, he was a good kisser.

When he had her a panting, mewling heap of need, he finally lifted his head. The fingers of one hand sifted through the hair at her shoulder. His eyes filled with a tenderness that made her shiver in spite of herself.

"Jeans off, but keep your underwear on. I'll do the same." He narrowed his eyes in playful sternness. "And no touching."

She let out a quiet laugh. "I promise."

"Good. You'll find out why we can't touch." He kissed her again, soft and lingering, then moved off her and rolled onto his back beside her. One corner of his mouth lifted. "You first."

She playfully rolled her eyes, but did as he asked. She was starting to think she wasn't the only one nervous about getting undressed. Keeping her gaze on his, she let the hunger in his eyes give her the courage to peel her jeans off. She'd never undressed in front of a man before, let alone him. By the time she tossed her jeans to the floor, she was shaking. With nerves. With an overwhelming sense of vulnerability.

"Your turn." She offered a smile, but it must have wobbled, because he leaned over her.

"Don't be nervous. It's just me." He pressed a tender kiss to her lips, then rolled onto his back.

She searched his face. "I could say the same thing, you know."

He stared for a moment, then frowned, deep grooves forming between his brows. "Is it that obvious that I'm stalling?"

She shrugged. "Only because I understand. May I ask why getting undressed in front of me makes you so nervous? Forgive the way this sounds, but I would have thought you'd be used to this part by now."

He drew a deep breath and blew it out, turning to stare at the ceiling. "I have a lot of scars. From the IED blast."

She took his chin in her hand and tilted his head until she could see his eyes. "They won't bother me."

"I appreciate that, but I haven't taken my shirt off in front of anyone but doctors and nurses since I came home." He finally looked over at her, vulnerability and uncertainty written in the lines of his face. "Going slow isn't just for you."

She wasn't the only one with insecurities, and seeing his made her heart ache for him. God help her. Her heart definitely wasn't coming away from this month unscathed.

"It's okay." She pressed a soft kiss to his shoulder, then hooked a finger into one of his belt loops and tugged. "Now stop stalling and take these off."

He let out a quiet laugh and gave her a two-fingered salute. "Yes, ma'am."

He lay back. Gaze locked on hers, he unbuttoned and unzipped his jeans. One corner of his mouth quirked upward, a playful gleam in his eyes as he slid them off and sent them sailing over the side of the bed. Then he mounded the pillows and scooted back to lean against the headboard. "Now we're even."

As it turned out, Trent wore old-fashioned boxers. Today's were plain white. The tent in the front made her mouth water. The thin cotton did little to hide his erection. Instead, the thin fabric seemed to outline the shape as it lay against his belly. Despite that long-ago conversation, she had no idea what average size was for a man, but Trent didn't seem small by any stretch of the imagination. The tip touched the waistband of his shorts. She knew from experience he was thick enough that her fingers wouldn't touch when she wrapped her hand around him.

Meeting his gaze, though, had her nervousness ramping up all over again. Now came the moment of truth. "How do you want me to lie?"

"Whatever's comfortable for you." Seeming to understand, he arched a brow. "Would like me to start?"

A hot flush rose up her neck and into her cheeks. She had to be red as a tomato by now. It was one thing to watch him do it, but another entirely to know he watched her. She'd never done this in front of anyone. Ever. "How is this even a turn-on for you? I'm so damn nervous I don't know what do with myself."

He slipped his hand into his boxers, cupped his erection, and stroked slowly. Base to tip judging by the movement of his hand. Her clit throbbed, her core aching. Holy mother of God that was hot.

"I actually like your inexperience. With you, there's no pretense. Your reactions are real." His hand moved again beneath his shorts, another slow stroke, then seemed to pause at the top. His jaw tightened, a quiet hissing leaving his mouth. "I'm right here with you. All the way."

She nodded and adjusted her position so that all she had to do was turn her head and she could see his eyes. He was right, of course. The way those blue eyes focused on hers eased the last of her nerves. The heat and hunger that filled them. The way his jaw tightened with every movement of his hand. Like he hung on by the barest, thinnest thread. It made her more than a little wet to know she affected him that way. No man had ever looked at her the way he was right now, and it flat-out awed her.

Her hand found its way into her panties, sliding into her slippery cleft. A single stroke over her clit sent pleasure shuddering through her. A soft moan escaped as every sensitive nerve ending came alive.

His nostrils flared, his chest heaving. "Are you wet?"

The little girl inside her who'd been taught sex before marriage was a sin said she ought to blush at his blatant question, but Lauren couldn't find the will to save her life. Of all the fantasies for him to fulfill, this one was huge. She loved the thought of his body against her, but she had no point of reference for sex to even understand what it felt like. Mutual masturbation, however, was easier to imagine. Stroking herself knowing he watched, getting to watch him do the same—the fantasy never failed to liquefy her insides. Actually playing it out, though?

"Very. It's hot and slippery and swollen." Every stroke of her fingers sent pleasure rippling through her, each wave stronger than the last. She was super sensitive, her body's reaction to him amped up by a thousand. "God, I want you."

"Let it go, doll. I'm honestly not sure how long I can hold off." He groaned and swore under his breath, his head banging back against the headboard. The tendons in his neck strained, his features taut with a mixture of arousal and torment. "This is torture, you know. Not getting to touch you. You got to touch last week. Saturday it's my turn."

His bold declaration only seemed to amp up the energy between them. They weren't even touching, yet they seemed to fuel each other. Every stroke of his hand, every time his breathing hitched and bliss traveled across his features, the ache deep inside increased to unbearable proportions. The faster she caressed herself, the faster his hand moved beneath his shorts.

Until the sounds of their need filled the silence. His harsh, erratic breathing. The quiet moans she couldn't contain. Her fingers flying over her slick flesh. The subtle creak of the springs as the bed rocked beneath them.

Pleasure built on top of pleasure, sending her rushing toward orgasm. Until she was gasping and panting, her hips bucking into the press of her fingers as her body sought relief for the desperate ache he'd created.

Her orgasm slammed into her out of nowhere. Muscles tightened and loosened as the bubble inside of her burst, flooding her every cell and leaving her gasping and breathless and feeling as if she were coming apart at the seams.

Trent let out a long groan that sounded torn from his chest, and she had the presence of mind to turn her head in time to watch his eyes slam shut. He'd thrown his head back against the headboard, and his mouth hung open in bliss. His hand had stopped moving, fingers cupped around the head of his penis, neatly capturing his seed, his belly quivering as he came. Just watching him had another orgasm washing through her, softer this time but no less euphoric.

Trent sank back against the headboard, chest heaving. "Jesus Christ."

As the throbbing faded to tiny aftershocks, Lauren could only lie there and try to remember to breathe. That he wasn't curling around her like last time made her chest tighten. Logically she understood it was because he needed to clean up, but it didn't make her feel any less open and exposed, like her protective outer shell had been ripped off to reveal a soft underbelly.

Last time they'd clung to each other. Now they were too separate. The lack of his body against her made Trent suddenly feel entirely too far away.

Seeming to understand something was off, he tilted her face to his and pressed a tender kiss to her lips. "I need to clean up. I'll be right back, okay?"

She nodded and watched as he left the room before turning to stare up at the ceiling. She was stupidly close to tears she couldn't begin to understand. All she knew was that vulnerability had a firm hold on her chest and wouldn't let go.

Trent returned a couple minutes later. He flicked the light off, then pulled down the covers and climbed onto the bed. He waited until she scooted beneath the covers herself; then he turned her onto her side. It wasn't until he curled against her back and tucked his hand beneath her body, holding her tightly against him, that the tension finally eased.

How in the world was she going to handle things when the month ended and they went back to being just friends? When he wouldn't hold her like this ever again?

He pressed his face into the back of her neck. "You're too quiet, doll. I can feel your tension. Talk to me."

"I…" She shook her head, unable to explain the tangle in her chest, then finally decided on simple. "Will you stay?"

"I'll stay. Though for the record, I would've only left if you'd asked me to."

She rolled onto her back so that she could look into his face, unable to hide her surprise. "Last time you said you couldn't handle us sleeping together."

He lifted a hand, stroking his fingers down her cheek, the touch tender and sweet. She closed her eyes, unable to help leaning her face into his palm. Conflicting emotions clutched at her chest. Warmth and affection, fear and a sense of bliss and safety. Oh, for sure she was losing her heart when this month ended because she was already falling in love with him.

"I know. I sent you home last week, and I hated it. It felt so wrong. I told you, I'm not that guy. I don't have to be at the shop until eight, so I'll have plenty of time to go home and shower. Just wake me when you get up." When she nodded, he kissed her gently, then closed his eyes. "Then it's settled. Sleep, doll. I'm not going anywhere."

CHAPTER TEN

Trent punched the doorbell, then leaned his hands on the frame, drumming his fingers on the wood. He hadn't slept worth a damn last night. Or the last two nights before that. He was tired and keyed up and the ghosts of his past wouldn't let him be. Carving hadn't helped. So he'd given up any pretense of productivity and had come to talk to Will and Skylar. What he sorely needed this morning was a dose of Will's sanity.

Despite being wealthy enough to buy an expansive home, Will and Sky owned a modest place overlooking Lake Washington. Three bedrooms, with a yard big enough for the dog they were always saying they'd get someday and a jungle gym for the kids they'd adopt. It was small and quaint and only a few miles from their parents' place.

The dead bolt turned with a quiet *clunk*, and Trent straightened off the frame in time for the door to swing open. It was a little past nine a.m., but like Trent, Will and Skylar had already been up for hours. Will was dressed, shaved, and ready for the day. As usual.

Will took one look at him and grinned. "Somebody's in the doghouse."

Trent furrowed his brow and shook his head. "Okay, you got me. What the hell about me even remotely tells you that?"

Will's grin only widened. "Because you look like something's eating at you. You haven't gotten that look since you've been home. You've been numb. And I'm just betting your problem is a woman. Mandy says you're seeing somebody."

Great. So everybody freaking knew.

"Who's in the doghouse?" Skylar came around the corner, looking between him and Will. At the sight of him, a grin spread across her face. Every bit as put together as Will, she sauntered to the door and punched Trent in the shoulder. "Don't give up there, tiger. She'll come around."

Trent glared at both of them, because he was pretty sure his face was red as a damn tomato. Will was about the only person he felt comfortable discussing his relationships with. Skylar, not so much. Oh, he knew Skylar would hear about it all anyway. He just didn't want to have to be the one to tell her. "This isn't exactly newsworthy stuff here."

Skylar, never one to miss an opportunity to taunt him, waggled her brows. "Is it Lauren?"

Trent folded his arms. "You guys 'bout done? I came over to talk about the party, not my sex life. I have an idea where to hold it. I wanted to run it by you before I set it into motion."

Still grinning like the cat that ate the canary, Will nodded toward the interior of the house. "Come on in. I'll get you some coffee."

"Thanks." Trent followed as Will wound his way through the foyer, past the living room, and into the kitchen, then dropped onto a stool at the breakfast bar.

Will crossed the space and pulled two mugs from a cabinet. He darted a glance over his shoulder as he reached for the coffeepot. "What's up?"

Trent folded his hands on the counter. "You want something low-key, just family and friends, right? What about Mom and Dad's? Big barbeque in the backyard. You know Mom would be thrilled."

Skylar came to stand beside him, resting her hands on the counter, and peered across the kitchen at Will. "I don't know about you, but I like the idea. It's intimate and personal, nothing flashy."

Skylar and her sisters came from honest roots, raised by a single father who'd lost his wife when the girls were small. That was partly what had the inspired the idea of the barbeque. Her father had died three years ago of a heart attack, and she'd confessed once to still missing him. He thought it might be nice if she felt surrounded by family.

Two steaming cups of coffee in hand, Will gave one to Skylar and set the other in front of Trent. "Yup. I like it." He rolled his eyes. "Mom will be over the moon. Don't bother hiring someone to cater."

Trent laughed and sipped at his coffee. "Because she won't let me. She'll insist on cooking. Yeah, I know. I'll see if I can wrangle Lauren into helping."

Skylar moved around the counter, pecked Will on the lips, and winked at Trent as she turned to leave the room. "I'll just leave you boys to *chat*."

When she finally disappeared around the doorway, Will laughed and moved back to the coffeepot, refilling his own mug. "You realize she's going to want the details later, right?"

Staring down into the dark liquid in his cup, Trent furrowed his brow and shook his head. "Yeah, I know. As long as I don't have to be the one to tell her. She gets far too much pleasure out of tormenting me."

Coffee mug in hand, Will chuckled as he slid onto the stool beside him. "Because she likes you. She thinks you're too serious."

Trent let out a sardonic laugh. "I am. Enough for both of us."

"Exactly." Will sipped at his coffee, turning to peer at Trent over the rim of his mug. "So what's really eating you? Thought things were going well with you and Lauren."

Trent set his elbows on the counter and ducked his head into his hands. "They are. That's exactly the problem. It's supposed to be just sex, but I find myself doing things I shouldn't."

Like going to see her because he couldn't resist the urge to simply be near her. When the shit in his head overwhelmed him, he craved her presence. He shouldn't have gone to the bakery three days ago, but the night before that had been hell. He'd spent most of it walking his apartment and craving her. He'd thought maybe if they had dinner, like they used to do before he'd gotten involved with her, then maybe he wouldn't feel so much like he was using her.

He dragged a hand through his hair. "It's going to end. It has to. I'm just not ready for more yet. This is all I can handle. Shouldn't I want more for her than this?"

Will nudged him with an elbow. "You need to stop thinking so damn much. If she's not complaining, then enjoy her while you have her."

Trent lifted his head and eyed his brother. "And if I hurt her?"

When he hurt her...

Will leveled him with a somber gaze. "She's the only person

you trust when that shit eats at you. You won't even come *here*." Will nudged him again. "If spending time with her gets you up and living, then run with it."

* * *

He was still stewing over his brother's words when his phone pinged several hours later. Seated on a bench at Chism Park, staring out over the calm waters of the lake, Trent released the heavy thoughts of AJ and fished his phone out of his pocket. A text from Lauren flashed across the screen.

Dinner at my place 2nite. I'll cook this time. Ur turn to bring dessert.

God, just the sight of her words on the screen inspired the image of her and set his heart hammering his rib cage. No doubt those words would have been spoken with a teasing clip. Those big brown eyes would have glinted with mischief, and damned if he didn't ache to kiss that smug smile off her face.

He punched in a quick reply. *Deal. What're u in the mood for? U ;)*

Trent groaned and reached down to adjust the hard-on springing to life in his jeans. He'd stroked himself to orgasm more than once over the last few days, giving in to the burning ache she'd inspired. The idea had been to take the edge off for their date, but she had only to toss something saucy at him and he was hard again. When she actually touched him later? Or looked at him through her lashes, in that innocent yet deliberate way she had? Christ. He'd be hard all damn night.

Nope. My turn 2night, remember? I have plans for you.

And he did. He'd spent far too much time pondering all the

ways he wanted to give her pleasure. He wanted to hear her call his name again right before her orgasm took her. Wanted to make her come so hard she forgot to breathe.

Then he wanted to do it all again. And again. And again.

Not fair. :(

Trent let out a quiet laugh and shook his head. Will was right; she flirted with him and thoughts of the war flitted away. *Dessert, doll. What're u in the mood 4?*

Surprise me.

Oh, he planned to.

Another message popped up before he could think of a response. *U at home?*

He darted a glance at the lake, watching the water lap at the shore. *No. At the park. Went for a run.*

Can you do that now?

He rolled his eyes. Of course she'd worry. *Yeah. Doc gave me the ok, long as I don't push 2 hard. Was slow and pathetic. Not even sure I worked up a sweat.*

I take it u didn't sleep well last nite?

How the hell she knew that, he hadn't a clue, but it was what had drawn him to her in the first place. She just seemed to understand, and that she did soothed the wound inside. Like she could heal all his broken parts.

No.

Ironically, he'd discovered he slept better next to her. So far he'd spent two nights in her bed, and twice she'd calmed the panic. He didn't dream any less, but more than once her scent insinuated itself into his nightmares, shifting the pain and confusion.

Not that he'd tell her that. Because he wasn't *supposed* to be sleeping with her. Not spending the night with her was *supposed* to keep those boundaries set firm.

But she kept annihilating his boundaries because he was weak when it came to her. She made him yearn for things he had no right to want. Team members who'd relied on him had died because he'd failed. Hell, he'd failed his marriage. What right did he have to be happy? To just live his life like nothing had happened? And what if he failed Lauren, too?

Firmly shoving *that* particular line of thinking aside, he punched in another quick reply. *What time u want me over?*

6?

Sounds good. See u in a few hours.

* * *

He'd ended up deciding on chocolate-covered strawberries for dessert, because he could feed them to her. Much like the truffles she'd brought by his place that first night.

When he showed up at her place—at six on the nose—and stood on her porch, waiting for her to open the door, he was hard again. Riffling through his head were memories of the last time he'd come over: watching her slip her hand into her panties, those heavy-lidded brown eyes locked on his when she came.

He shoved a hand through his hair. If he made it through dinner without peeling her clothing off it would be a miracle.

When she opened the door, his heart flat-out stalled. Lauren, apparently, had dressed to kill. She wore those jeans that hugged her curves, but her top gained the full attention of every inch of his body. The deep V neckline went clear down between her breasts, the fabric knotted there to draw his attention. More than a little of her breasts mounded along the neckline. The long sleeves had slits that exposed her soft shoulders, making his mouth water with the overwhelming desire to bend his head and taste her creamy skin.

"Wow." He swallowed in a vain attempt to wet his desert-dry throat and forced his gaze off her chest.

A beautiful soft pink suffused her cheeks, and she glanced down at herself. "I told Steph I had a date tonight. She loaned me this."

He was over the threshold and wrapping himself around her before he'd even realized he'd moved. He set the box of strawberries onto a side table and braced a hand against her lower back. With the other, he followed the V of that neckline. "You realize this is more of you than I've ever seen."

She shivered in his arms, a whisper-soft breath leaving her mouth. "I wanted something a bit more provocative for tonight. Something sexy I thought you'd like."

He couldn't stop the quiet groan that left him and tightened his hold on her, drawing her impossibly closer until he was taking every breath with her and he could feel the pounding of her heart against his chest. "Doll?"

Her long lashes fluttered as she lifted her gaze to his. "Yeah?"

"You could've shown up in those flannel pajamas of yours." He shook his head and, unable to resist, brushed his mouth over hers. She leaned into him, her soft lips slanting over his, and what started as a simple greeting quickly became hot and heavy. She wound her arms around his neck and pushed her breasts into his chest. Her tongue snaked into his mouth, bold as brass, and he was lost. In her.

When they finally parted, both were breathless. He let out a quiet, torture-filled laugh and dropped his forehead to hers. "You realize we're never making it through dinner, right?"

Another flush rose into her cheeks. "I'm sorry. I know we're supposed to take this slow, but I haven't stopped thinking about you all day."

There it was, that soft, uncertain side of her, the innocent virgin who called to something primal within him, who made him ache to protect her at all costs.

Christ. He was in a sinking ship and going down fast.

"Me either." He nipped at her bottom lip. "Ask me how many hard-ons I've had to try to ignore today. It's why I went for a run this morning. A cold shower wasn't cutting it."

She shivered again and closed her eyes. Her chest rose and fell at an increased pace, her erratic breaths puffing against his lips. "I thought about you last night."

He groaned. He didn't have to ask to know she was telling him she'd touched herself. Made herself come while thinking of him.

He stepped further into the house and shut the door behind him. Then he leaned back against the foyer wall, pulling her with him. "Tell me."

Leaning on his chest now, she opened her eyes and caught his gaze. Hers filled with a heat that burned him up from the inside out. "I was lying in bed, thinking about Tuesday night. Watching you stroke your...cock."

That word from her sweet mouth had said member trying to escape its confinement. He was pretty sure it was leaking already. Never in all the years he'd known her had he ever heard her use that word or anything like it. Not even that day he'd caught her and Mandy discussing penis size. Hearing it now was like dousing a fire with gasoline. She may as well have lit his damn fuse.

He closed his eyes, unable to stop the shudder that moved through him. Nor could he stop himself from asking. "You're killing me, babe. And?"

Her breath whispered over his mouth. "And I ached. Found myself lying there, staring at the ceiling, rubbing my nipples. God, remembering the look on your face when you came made me so wet."

He groaned, the vision filling his mind. Her on her bed, thighs spread, fingers flying over her slippery flesh. It didn't help that he knew exactly what she looked like when she stroked herself to orgasm. "So you eased the ache."

She leaned in closer, so that when she spoke, her lips moved against his, her voice so low he had to focus to hear her. "You made me lose my breath, Trent. And you weren't even there."

"Shit." He dropped his head back, banging it against the wall behind him. "I know I asked, but please, for the love of my sanity, no more. Or I'm going to come in my damn jeans."

She let out a quiet, breathy laugh and pushed off his chest. "Come on. Let's go see about dinner. I cooked. We should at least attempt to eat."

* * *

Trent set the last glass into the dishwasher and closed the door. Beside him, Lauren had gotten out the strawberries and was currently whipping some fresh cream to go with them. Frustration wound through him as he leaned back against the counter to watch her.

Sitting through dinner was a cross somewhere between heaven and hell. He enjoyed the simplicity of sitting with her and sharing a meal. She was a fantastic cook. She'd made pasta and garlic bread. Simple, but delicious because he knew damn well she'd made it all from scratch.

The tension between them he could've cut up and served for dessert. Sitting in her dining room making small talk had been painful. Neither of them had been able to focus much on anything but the after-dinner fun. She'd take a bite and ask about something inane, like his current project at work, then peek up at him between her lashes or set that damn fork in her mouth and pause, waiting for a response he wasn't capable of giving her. He couldn't think about anything but waiting to watch the steel tines drag between her lips as she pulled that fork from her mouth. He was hard all through dinner. By the time she pulled the wire whisk from the frothy cream, he was ready to bust through his zipper.

Lauren turned, seeming to head for the sink, tongue flicking out to swipe a bit of cream off the end of the whisk. At the sight of him, she froze, pulling her tongue back into her mouth. Eyes wide and filling with heat, she stood and stared.

Trent groaned, pulled the utensil from her hand and set it in the sink. Then he hooked her around the waist and tugged her against him. He slid his hands to her ass, allowed himself a moment to relish the firm, supple muscle. "If I have to watch you eat one more thing, I'll go insane."

A soft pink flush stained her cheeks as she dropped her gaze to his chest. "I was trying to take things slow."

"I appreciate that." He lifted a hand, caressing her cheek with the backs of his fingers. "But you're killing me."

She let out a quiet laugh.

"I'm putting you in charge tonight." Unable to help himself, he stroked his thumb along her bottom lip. "What do you want, Lauren?"

She slid her hands around his rib cage and up his back, pressing so close her breath whispered over his mouth. "You."

He smiled. "How?"

"You said I got to touch last time and it was your turn tonight." She studied him for a moment before drawing a shuddering breath. "That's what I want. For you to touch me this time. To use your fingers."

His mind filled with the memory of that first night in her apartment, when she'd told him what she thought about when she masturbated. A groan worked its way out.

"God, you make my cock ache when you talk like that. Come on." He brushed a kiss across her mouth, then took her hand and led her into the bedroom.

Once there, he crawled up on the bed and pulled her down with him, rolling her beneath him. She slid her hands up his back, but stared at him for a moment, eyes searching his. Like she had something on her mind.

He traced the shell of her ear, tucking a thick lock of hair. "What?"

"I have one request."

"Okay." Not only was she indulging his need to go slow, but she seemed to enjoy it. He had to give her this one.

"Take your shirt off?"

His gut tightened. The moment of truth. And he wasn't any less nervous about this.

Her soft fingers caressed his cheek. Like somehow she knew, understood what he couldn't bring himself to tell her. "I just want to see you, to touch you."

He sighed. "You know it's not you, right?"

She studied him for a moment, then sat upright, forcing him to move off her. As he rolled onto his back, she shifted onto her knees. He didn't miss the way her hands trembled. His own were doing something very similar. She looked him right in the eye, though, as she gripped the hem of her shirt and pulled it over her head. One corner of her mouth lifted as she tossed it la-di-da style over the side of the bed.

"There." She tugged on the end of his shirt. "Your turn. Unless you'd rather I take it off for you?"

That had merit, actually.

He pulled himself upright and shifted onto his knees, then held his arms out from his sides. "Be my guest."

Heat flared in her eyes as she shuffled toward him. They were belly to belly now, the luscious aroma of her perfume floating around him, and her erratic breaths teased his lips. The first touch of her warm hands on his bare skin wrenched a groan out of him.

"You have the softest hands." His eyes closed on a ragged exhalation. One touch and she had him on his knees, literally *and* figuratively. He couldn't stop picturing those heavenly hands wrapped around his cock.

She stroked her palms upward, taking his shirt with them. Up his belly. Over his pecs. The quiet little *hmmm* she let out, like she took immense pleasure in doing only that, nearly undid him. "And *you're* warm. God, this is so much better than the fantasy."

He gritted his teeth until his jaw ached. Those words pulled all rational thought from his brain. God, how he ached to be inside her. To pin her beneath him and slide into her velvet heat. "You keep teasing me with stuff like that, doll, and I'm going to lose what little self-control I have."

A soft, shuddering breath left her, and she dropped her forehead to his chest, a shiver running through her that set fire to his blood. "Touch me."

He growled low in his throat and turned his head, raking his teeth over her earlobe. Then he leaned back and held her gaze. He started with her bra. It was sexy. Black lace. See-through cups that allowed him to see her nipples.

It was in the way. It hit the floor in seconds, and he couldn't help himself. He cupped her in his hands, stroking his thumbs over her tightened nipples before he'd thought about what part of her he *wanted* to touch first.

The quiet moan she let out sent a wave of fire straight to his groin. He groaned and bent his head, sucking one puckered tip into his mouth. She moaned again, her fingers sliding along his scalp, encouraging him.

Blind with the need to feel her, all of her, against him, he shifted to lie on the bed, pulling her down with him. She laid along his length, her weight slight but welcome, and stared. Something moved between them, silent but aching, and the tension between them snapped. She braced her hands on his chest and pushed upright, straddling his hips like she knew exactly what to do.

For a moment all he could do was watch her. Beautiful. She was so fucking beautiful sitting over him like that. She had perky breasts, high and proud, nipples jutting up and outward. Her long dark hair was a curtain around her face as her trembling fingers moved to the button on his jeans.

He shackled her wrist, shaking his head as he rolled her over, then leaned down and claimed her mouth for a tender kiss. "My turn to touch, remember?"

Despite the erratic hammering of his heart, he forced himself to go slow. To enjoy the suppleness of her skin, that intoxicating scent clinging to her as he kissed and caressed his way down her body. He stopped to pay homage to each breast. Sucked on the tips. Kneaded them in his hands and lightly pinched her nipples. Once again she let out a quiet, agonized moan and slid her fingers along his scalp.

Then he kissed his way down her soft belly. When he reached her jeans, he peered up at her, asking the silent question. Was she sure?

She nodded, and his erection twitched in his jeans. If it were possible to be any more aroused…Jesus. He was shaking so much he fumbled over the button. Turned out she wore a matching pair of lace panties. They were pretty, but like the bra, they were in the way. They hit the floor along with her bra and jeans.

She was naked before him now, and he took a moment to drink her in. She was long and lean and so beautiful. He stroked his fingers over her hips, her thighs, enjoying the feel of her beneath his hands, that he could even touch her like this at all. The idea had been to use his hands to make her come, but her nakedness before him called to him like a siren's song.

He finally gave in and sifted his fingers through the short curls at the apex of her thighs. Damned if he could help himself. "You don't wax."

"I'm sorry. Is it a turnoff?"

"No. Just the opposite." It made his mouth water. It had been a long damn time since he'd been with a woman who took pride in her body exactly the way it was. Wendy had always insisted on a landing strip, as she called it. Hell, she'd even bedazzled the damn thing. Lauren's neatly trimmed curls were arousing as hell.

Then and there he nixed the idea of touching. He didn't want to touch. He wanted to *taste*. He wanted the flavor of her on his tongue.

When he shifted to lie on his belly between her thighs, Lauren reached down, attempting to pull him back up. "You don't have to do that. You said touching."

The unease in her voice had him jerking his head up. Lauren stared at the ceiling, her face flushed, body stiff as a two-by-four.

He stroked a hand over her belly. "Why does this make you uneasy?"

She shook her head. "Steph said most men don't like to. You said touching tonight…"

He grunted in disgust. "That's because Steph's dating the wrong kinds of men. Some of us happen to enjoy it." To prove his point, he leaned in and inhaled, drawing in her scent, then groaned. "God you smell good."

She smelled like a woman. Clean. Musky.

He dipped his head again, this time stroking her sensitive folds with a long swipe of his tongue. Lauren let out a strangled gasp, her hips arching upward. That one tiny reaction fueled his need. Shaking now, he went in again, another long taste, pushing his tongue into her. She moaned softly, this one agonized. When he sucked her clit into his mouth, her body went limp, thighs dropping open as she finally relaxed into the bed.

Out the corner of his eye, he watched her fingers curl against the comforter again. "Oh God…"

That sound, soft and throaty and full of sweet agony, stoked the flame in his belly to a full-body burn, and he lost whatever control he had. He wanted her to come and hard. Over and over and over.

So he slid his hands beneath the firm globes of her ass and lifted her to his mouth. He reveled in the sweet taste of her. In the way her body responded to his ministrations. Lauren gasped and sighed, wonder in her breathy voice. Her belly and thighs began to shake and her hands clenched and unclenched around the comforter beneath her.

He knew she was close when her legs stiffened and she gripped his head, pulling him in tighter. She came with a gentle bucking of her hips, riding his mouth like she owned him.

Trent didn't release her or let her up. He kept at her, licking and sucking, taking all she gave and demanding more. He couldn't help himself. She was so fucking beautiful, back arched, body shaking like she'd lost all control of herself. To know he was the one who'd made her come undone like that? Jesus. He wanted to beat his damn chest. It was selfish to think, but the sight was addicting all the same.

When she finally collapsed back into the bed and closed her legs, he kissed her belly and shifted to lie down beside her. His erection throbbed painfully, and just the sensation of his shorts gliding against the engorged head, combined with her body heat against him, was almost too much. It had taken all his self-control not to come with her that last time. He had enough presence of mind to gather her to him, but all he could do for a moment was remember to drag in oxygen.

Lauren slid her hand up his chest, soft fingers sifting through the hair in the center, and purred like a contented cat. She tilted her head enough to meet his gaze, big brown eyes liquid and soft, and smiled. "Your turn."

CHAPTER ELEVEN

Lauren slid over of Trent. Straddling his hips, she reached for the button on his jeans with trembling fingers. "I have to warn you, I've never done this before."

She caught the words too late to suck them back. Of course he knew that. Because she'd told him exactly how inexperienced she was. But she was completely out of her element again and babbling.

She rolled her eyes and glanced up, ready to admit all of that to him, when his expression caught her. Trent lay glaring at the ceiling. "What?"

He turned that frown on her, his gaze searching her face. After a moment he let out a heavy sigh and jerked his back to the ceiling. "I'm glad you've never done this before, because I hate the thought of you doing it for anyone else."

Her heartbeat hitched, one corner of her mouth lifting in response. This was just sex. Logically, she knew that. She wasn't naive enough to think this would end in anything but heartbreak. Neither could she resist. She wanted the time she had with him, and his very evident jealousy made her chest swell. Deep down inside, it made her feel the tiniest bit like she was *his*.

She dropped her gaze to his belly and tugged the button of his jeans open. "It's going to happen, you know. This is going to end, and we're both going to see other people. That was part of the deal."

In two seconds flat she found herself on her back. Trent pinned her to the bed with his hips, his erection pressing against her core. He bent his head to her throat, his voice low and gruff in her ear as he skimmed his mouth along her jaw. "But for the next two weeks, you're *mine*. Don't forget that part."

"Trent?" She reached between them and pulled down his zipper, making sure her fingers brushed his erection as she did.

He froze above her, lips pausing on a stroke over the muscle of her shoulder. She didn't miss the tremor that moved through him. "Hmm?"

She slid her hand inside his pants, palming his erection. She had no clue what a man was supposed to feel like, but she loved the firm, softness of him. "That's the part I like. Those were your rules. Not mine."

He lifted his head, his irritation gone. Now his eyes were tender, filling with an intimacy that caught her in the chest. That look in his eyes nudged the part of her that wanted…more. With him.

He brushed his mouth over hers. "I like that part, too."

She rose and rolled him onto his back. Straddling his hips once again, she leaned over him and nipped at his bottom lip. "My turn."

Following his lead, she kissed her way down his chest, stopping occasionally to kiss the shrapnel scars, before moving down his belly. She kissed the skin above his jeans, then gripped the waistband in her hands and kissed her way down his legs as she pulled them off.

Halfway down, the scar on his right thigh caught her attention. Having long since healed over, it was little more than a red line running the length of his thigh. The memory of the cast he'd worn for six weeks filled her mind. She brushed her lips along the scar before finally pulling his jeans and underwear off and tossing them over the side of the bed.

He was now fully naked, and she sat back on her heels, allowing herself a moment to look at him. He really was beautifully made, lean and muscular. His cock lay stiff against his belly. It twitched beneath her gaze, and she glanced at him to find him watching her, those blue eyes blazing.

She crawled up the bed, kneeling between his spread legs. Her hands began to shake again as she stroked them up his thighs and over his hips. "Any advice?"

He let out a soft laugh, the fingers of his right hand sifting into her hair. "Yeah. Don't bite me."

She wanted to laugh, too, but butterflies had ahold of her stomach. Rather, she peered up at him, feeling entirely too helpless. Was she ruining the moment? "I'm serious."

His fingers caressed the back of her head. "Relax, Lauren. You can't possibly get this wrong. Just go with what feels right. I'll warn you before I come. If you don't want a mouthful, you should stop at that point."

Yeah. Steph had warned her about that, too.

Heart hammering like a freight train, she nodded, settled on her belly between his legs, and let her need to please him fuel her movements. The orgasm he'd given her this way had been off the charts. She wanted to blow his mind. So she took her time caressing his length, enjoying the feel of him in her hand. His body trembled against her, his breath hitching.

When she finally enveloped him in her mouth, he let out a low, guttural groan, the hand in her hair fisting. "Slow. Ohh, Christ, go slow. You have me so wound up."

She had to admit she enjoyed everything about this. The feel of him in her mouth. The flavor of his skin. Even the slightly salty tang that erupted on her taste buds. It was his reactions, however, that fueled the fire raging in her stomach. Every soft stroke drew a reaction out of him. His belly jumped. His trembling escalated. His breaths soughed in and out of his mouth.

So she increased her pace, working her hands along with her mouth. She *needed* his pleasure.

He let out a low, deep groan and reached for her, groping blindly until he gripped her shoulder. "Doll…come off. Come off…"

Remembering his warning, she popped him from her mouth, glancing up at him as she stroked him with her hand. He groaned, fingers digging into her skin, mouth hanging open in bliss, eyes squeezed tightly shut. His seed rocketed out of the pulsing tip, splashing his chest and quivering belly.

Okay, so she got it, why he'd insisted on doing this for her. In the grips of an orgasm, he was truly beautiful to behold. It took a lot of trust to let someone do that, and his vulnerability in that moment awed her.

He went limp, body relaxing finally into the mattress. A long breath left him in a rush, as if he'd been holding it, and he let his hands flop to his sides. "Jesus Christ."

Again she followed his lead and kissed a clean spot on his belly before climbing up to lie beside him.

He opened his eyes and turned his head, leaning over to brush a kiss across her mouth. "You are fucking incredible."

His hand found hers, where it rested on the bed between them, long fingers threading through hers, and she leaned her head against his shoulder. They lay in comfortable silence, just the sounds of his labored breathing filling the room.

"Trent?"

"Hmm?"

"I actually enjoyed that."

"Me too." He let out a breathless laugh and pressed a kiss to her forehead, then rested his head against hers, his voice an intimate hum between them. "I'd hold you, but I'm a mess. I'll be right back."

She watched him leave the room before getting up long enough to move beneath the covers. As she lay staring at the ceiling, the sheets cool against her bare skin, her chest tightened with a mixture of pleasure and pain, swelling and aching at the same time. She might not have forever with him, but she could never regret this. If this was all the time she'd have with him, she'd take it.

He came back a couple minutes later, crawled into the bed beside her and curled against her back. She drifted off to sleep with his arm around her waist, holding her so tightly she might as well have been a second skin.

* * *

Trent woke the next morning with the sun. Lying on his side, he took a moment to drink in the sight beside him. Lauren lay on her back, mouth slack in slumber, breathing deep and even, gloriously, beautifully naked. The covers had slipped down, now lying around her waist, and her nipples puckered in the cool air of the morning. He couldn't resist tracing a finger over her right breast, following the curve up and over those perky, dusky nipples.

She shivered and moaned softly in her sleep, rolling onto her side to face him.

This. This was the feeling he missed, waking to a warm body and supple, feminine curves. That the body was Lauren's only made the moment sweeter.

It also increased the soul-deep ache in his chest. He yearned to make love to her, but the why had changed a bit. He wanted to connect to her on every possible level, to take a piece of her with him when he had to end this side of their relationship.

And he did have to end it. He firmly reminded himself why every time this feeling crept over him. These days, he felt it a lot. It seeped over his chest, a sense of loneliness that ate away at his soul. They'd been together like this for only two weeks, but it seemed like a lifetime.

Which was why he was getting out of this damn bed.

Twenty minutes later, he was dressed in his jeans and halfway through making breakfast when Lauren appeared in the kitchen entrance. In a light pink terry-cloth bathrobe and fuzzy slippers, of all things, she shuffled into the room. Her hand slid across the bare skin of his back as she stopped beside him and peered around his shoulder at the stove. "Do you ever sleep late?"

Despite the brewing coffee and the aroma of cooking bacon that permeated the air, his senses focused on her. Warm skin. A hint of her musky perfume. God, he ached to bury his mouth between her thighs again. To bend his head and find that sensitive spot on her shoulder that made her shiver.

He tossed her a smile and prayed it looked at least somewhat realistic. "Not really. Habit, I suppose."

She peered up at him, head tilted back slightly to meet his gaze. Her eyes were soft and filled with a mischief that made him ache all over. "I was hoping to wake up next to you this morning."

He forced a laugh and concentrated on pulling the cooked bacon from the pan, laying the pieces on the small rack to drain. If he didn't, he'd be turning to her. "I think it's better for both of us that I got out of bed. If I had stayed, that rule to wait to make love would've ended this morning."

Lauren let out a quiet laugh and slid behind him, pressing a kiss to his back as her warm hands slid up his chest. "That was your rule, not mine. You wouldn't have heard me complaining."

His gut clenched. She wouldn't have, and he damn well knew it, but that wasn't why he'd gotten up.

"I need you too much. I'm not sure I would've been gentle." That wasn't entirely a lie, but it wasn't the whole truth either. After sleeping beside her naked curves all night, he'd woken with the hard-on to end all hard-ons. Jesus, he couldn't remember the last time he'd wanted a woman this bad.

He'd also needed some semblance of distance, time to get those boundaries straight in his head. To remind himself why he'd made them. He'd failed Wendy as a husband. Had failed Cooper and AJ. And if he let himself fall for Lauren, he'd fail her, too. He would *not* lose her. She was the sunshine in his world, and the day she walked out of it was the day he had to go back to living in the dark. As friends, she'd remain in his life.

He turned the burner off and slid the hot frying pan aside, then turned, resting his hands on the counter's edge as he leaned back against it. "Got any plans for the day?"

"Nope." She flashed a smile that melted as quickly as it appeared and laid a hand against his chest, eyes searching his. "You okay?"

"I'm fine. I just wanted to make you breakfast." That at least was true. To distract her from this line of questioning, he pressed a tender kiss to her lips. "I'd like you to sit for me."

The idea had hit him as he lay watching her sleep. She was beautiful and he wanted a memento to remember her by.

Her eyes widened with surprise. "You want to carve *me*?"

He nodded once. "In the nude, if that's okay."

Her brows shot up into her hairline, but one side of her mouth hitched. "Nude?"

"Do you mind?" He wasn't sure he could explain it if he had to. Each carving represented something, some bit of pain. She was a bright spot, and he wanted something that would serve as proof that she'd once been his.

She grinned full out now and swirled a pointed finger over his chest. "And exactly where will this carving go?"

He winked. "In my bedroom, of course."

Desire flared in her eyes, and just that fast, he was hard again, his cock pressing painfully against his zipper. Her warm hands slid up his chest like a seductive caress as she pressed her curves into him, lifted onto her toes, and leaned so close her lips brushed his as she spoke. "Shower with me first."

He groaned as the last of his willpower snapped. He untied the sash of her robe—because he was dying to know what, if anything, she wore beneath it—and pulled the sides open.

"Christ. You're still naked." His hands gained a mind of their own, seeking out all that warm, supple skin.

"And you're not." She shivered, her hands trembling as she slid them down his chest and belly to the button on his jeans. One tug and she had them open. A flick of her wrist and the zipper went with it. When she slid her hand inside, warm, soft fingers curling around his erection, he cursed under his breath.

He dropped his head back and closed his eyes. "Have mercy, doll."

Just as quickly, she pulled away and took his hand instead. He opened his eyes in time for her to tug him away from the counter.

He shook his head. "Lauren...breakfast..."

"Will wait." She shot a coy smile over her shoulder, and for a moment he could only follow in stunned silence as she led him down the hallway into the bathroom. Once there, she released his hand and moved to the shower to start the water.

Then she faced him, that smoky gaze pinned on his as she slid the robe from her shoulders, where it pooled at her feet. She let him look a moment before crossing the small space with a seductive sashay of her hips. Apparently taking no prisoners, she didn't wait for him to finish undressing, but gripped the waistband of his jeans and boxers, taking them with her as she knelt at his feet.

When she peered up at him, he nearly came. Lauren Hayes was kneeling at his damn feet, eye to eye, as it were, with his throbbing erection. It didn't help that she leaned in and drew her tongue up his length.

When she pushed to her feet again, he growled low in his throat and hooked her around the waist, tugging her against him. Her naked body hit his, trapping his aching cock against the lush softness of her belly, but he managed to somehow hold on to himself and instead nipped at her bottom lip. "Tease. You sure are feeling your oats this morning."

Lauren froze, that sassiness fading. Her eyes widened in uncertainty. "When I woke without you this morning, I decided to come find you and drag you back to bed."

He dropped his forehead to hers. She slayed him. She honestly did. In two seconds flat, she had him on his knees at her feet. "I'm sorry. I just needed a little time to myself this morning."

Her warm palm settled against his chest. "You *didn't* sleep well."

He drew and released a heavy breath. "Same damn dream. It's like waking up in the hospital that first time all over again. I'm always disoriented, and then there you were. I'm not sure I can tell you how much I needed you this morning."

She sifted her fingers through the hair on his chest, voice low, soothing, understanding. "I wouldn't have stopped you. I would've welcomed it."

His head rocked against hers. "I couldn't have been gentle with you. Not then."

He'd ached to roll on top of her and sink into her, to surround himself in everything about her. Her musky, flowery perfume, her silky heat, her soft bare curves. But it would have been hard and fast and brutal. He wouldn't have been able to restrain himself. His need right then had been too great. One touch from her always seemed to right his world again, and he'd needed to immerse himself in her.

To fuck her until he stopped feeling like he was coming apart at the seams, because in her arms he was beginning to feel... whole again.

"I won't use you that way."

"You're too much of a gentleman for your own good, Trent." She pressed a kiss to his chest, then stepped back and took his hand, turning to the shower. "Come on. I have just the thing for you."

He stepped out of his jeans and boxers, leaving them on the floor, and she pulled him into the shower with her, then shut the glass doors. She pushed him back beneath the warm spray, and for a moment, stood looking at him. She made him feel transparent, and what she saw didn't seem to scare her a damn bit.

Lauren leaned over, picking up a bottle of body wash he was sure would make him smell like a woman all day, and squirted some onto her palm. She rubbed her hands together, then spread the soap over his chest, down his belly. He stood, caught in her eyes, watching her, enjoying the simple glide of her soft hands over him. When she slid those soapy fingers around his length, his knees nearly buckled from under him.

"Fuck." He squeezed his eyes shut, his blood roaring in his ears, his entire body trembling.

She pressed her breasts into his chest, her whisper-soft breaths teasing his lips. "What do you need?"

He clenched his jaw until he was sure his teeth would crack. "You."

"That's not what I asked." She leaned closer, her voice an intimate whisper as she leaned her mouth to his ear. "Let me help. Tell me what you need."

The tenderness in her voice sapped the last of his reserves. He braced his hands on the shower wall behind her and dropped his forehead onto her shoulder. "Hard and fast. Don't be gentle."

Her slippery hands began to move then. Lauren didn't pull any punches, either, but did exactly as he'd asked—tightened her grip and pumped her hand. She leaned her cheek against his head, her voice a vulnerable, tender murmur in his ear. She was panting as hard as he was. "Like this?"

All he could do was grunt in acknowledgment, because her hands hadn't stopped moving. His orgasm slammed into him from out of nowhere, and he came with a low growl that felt torn from deep within.

When it ended, he could only stand for a moment, dragging in oxygen. He leaned his forehead against hers. "Thank you."

True to her generous nature, she gave him a tender smile and stroked his cheek. "You're welcome. Being human is allowed, you know."

He gripped her face in his hands, telling her everything he couldn't find the words to say by sealing his mouth over hers. He kissed her harder than he probably should have, but she flat-out fucking amazed him, and he could think of only one way to show her.

When they finally parted, they were both breathless. Determined to make it up to her, he squirted a generous amount of soap in his hands, rubbed them together, and went about washing *her*. Over her shoulders and down her arms. Over her belly and hips and around to her ass. He paid particular attention to her breasts, massaging them in his palms, stroking her tightened nipples.

Then he turned her to face the opposite direction, pulled her back against him, and slid his hand between her thighs. With one hand on a breast, playing with her nipple, he slipped his fingers of the other hand into her hot folds.

She let out a blissful sigh and dropped her head back on his shoulder, already shivering. He bent his head to her neck, kissing her throat, her shoulder, any part of her he could reach, all the while stroking her swollen clit. Every caress had her going more and more limp against him, until she was shaking and panting and pushing against the press of his fingers.

When she finally erupted, she let out a soft cry that simultaneously filled his soul and made him want to beat his chest. Her knees buckled, and he gripped her waist hard, supporting her as he continued to caress her, desperate to make the pleasure last as long as he could for her.

She finally went limp against him and let out a breathless laugh, her hand gripping his hard. "God. Thank you."

He chuckled and kissed her cheek. "Just returning the favor. You want to know why I want to carve you? Because you amaze me. Spend the day with me. We'll go over to my place, and you can lie naked on my sofa while I carve you. Then maybe you'll be lunch."

She shivered. "I like that idea. Can you do it all in one day?"

"I doubt it. But I can probably get your general shape down. I'd like to take pictures, too, if that's all right."

She twisted at the waist, peering over her shoulder at him. One dark brow arched in bemusement. "You want naked pictures of me."

He chuckled. "To use as a guide after you go home. Unless you want to sit naked on my sofa until I'm finished?"

Mischief glinted in her eyes. "If you promise to make me come like that again when you're done, I'd sit there a whole damn week."

He brushed his mouth over hers. "Then it's a date."

CHAPTER TWELVE

Posing in the nude had to be the most erotic thing she'd ever done. Also the most nerve-racking. An hour later, Lauren stood naked as the day she was born in the center of Trent's living room. Her nerves were shot. Every limb shook.

After drying each other off and getting dressed, they'd finished breakfast before making their way to his apartment on the other side of town. Upon arriving at his place, he'd set up his workbench, which sat on the far-right wall of the living room, and laid a flat, three-foot-by-five-foot piece of wood on the surface. Then he'd asked her to undress.

He now studied her with intense scrutiny, as if she were a work of art. She supposed she was to him at this moment, but his gaze seemed to penetrate, made her skin tingle and her stomach do somersaults. Undressing in front of him when they were intimate, distracted by his wandering hands and heady kisses, was one thing. Watching him dissect her bits and parts was another entirely.

She twisted her hands together. "Where do you want me?"

His gaze finally refocused on hers. Those blue eyes searched her face for a moment before he crossed the space between them, hooked her around the waist, and pulled her close.

"Don't be nervous. It's just me." He caressed the back of his fingers along her cheek and inclined his head, indicating behind her. "Lie down on the sofa and get comfortable. I've turned the heat up a bit, but if you get cold or you just need a break, let me know, okay?"

She nodded, and he brushed his mouth over hers, then released her and stepped back. She tried to do as he asked, to find a position that made her feel sexy, but all she felt was awkward and way too aware of her every imperfection. "Like this?"

"Relax, doll." He dropped to his knees beside her and bent his head to her breast, enveloping the puckered tip in the warmth of his mouth.

Pleasure flooded over the surface of her skin and Lauren gasped, arching her back. Seeming to know exactly what she wanted and needed, he cupped her in his palm, massaging and kneading and suckling. In seconds flat, he had her shivering, her thighs spreading, the ache in her core building to unbearable proportions.

What she wanted—needed—was his fingers back between her thighs, stroking and exploring…

She shifted her restless legs over the sofa, tried to arch her hips to make some sort of contact. "Touch me. Please."

Trent pulled away instead, sat back on his heels and scanned her body.

"Much better." He tapped her lips with his index finger. "Now don't move."

Then he rose to his feet and returned to his workbench.

She sagged into the cushions and playfully glared at his back. "Tease."

He chuckled and picked up a tool, then twisted at the waist, peering back at her with that intense, focused gaze. "Seriously. Stay just like that. I promise I'll make it up to you, but I wanted you to relax."

He was right, though. Damn him. It worked. Her nervousness was gone. Except now she was wet, and her clit throbbed. Well, two could play at that game.

Taking her cues from him, she ran the tips of her fingers around her nipples, idly circling them. His nostrils flared, and Trent drew a deep breath, his gaze glued to her fingers. So she cupped her breasts in her hands and massaged them the way he had. Glancing down his body, Lauren watched a distinctive bulge form behind his zipper.

She hoped he'd come back and finish what he'd started. Instead, Trent cocked his head to the side, studying her as if suddenly seeing her differently. After a moment, he nodded. "Touch yourself."

Her heartbeat skipped. It took all of two seconds for her to realize what, exactly, he meant. "Surely you aren't going to carve *that*."

He returned to the sofa and dropped to his knees beside her. His gaze traveled her body, his hand following, caressing her curves. Over her belly. Down her hip. Along the front of her left thigh. "You're beautiful, and your little display there inspired me. Close your eyes. What's your favorite fantasy?"

Every inch of her tingled in response, her skin coming alive beneath his touch. The answer to his question was too easy. "You. Watching you stroke your cock."

Oh yeah, she'd said that word on purpose. She'd noted his reaction the last time she'd said it, the surprised, hungry gleam in his eyes. If he planned to torture her, she'd get hers.

He groaned and leaned down, capturing her mouth, a luscious tangle of lips and tongues and softly biting teeth. Just enough to make her want. To make her arch her back, desperate for him to touch her again.

Like last time, though, Trent pulled back. "I had plans to bury my mouth between your thighs when I was done, but all right. Do this for me, and I'll let you watch again."

The thought made her clit pulse in delicious anticipation. Her hands wandered down her stomach, slipping into her drenched folds. She caressed her aching clit with the tip of a finger, enough to light her body on fire. To tease *him*. "Let me watch now."

She *hoped* he'd cave. She should have known better.

While a bonfire lit in those gorgeous eyes, Trent turned his mouth to her ear, soft lips she knew damn well felt incredible between her thighs teasing her skin as he spoke. "Make yourself come, Lauren. I want to capture that, how fucking beautiful you are when you relax and let yourself go."

The husky tone of his voice had her body liquefying and melting into the sofa cushions. She couldn't deny him if she tried. Giving in, she nodded, and he brushed a soft kiss across her mouth.

"Thank you." He pushed to his feet and returned to his bench.

Lauren closed her eyes and immersed herself in the fantasy. The memory of his hand on his stiff member. How long and beautiful he was. The sounds of his arousal. The scent of it that filled the air. Every image that flooded her mind took her back to that moment, and her fingers flew in a desperate rush for relief over her aroused flesh. Despite that she was naked, heat erupted along her skin. Her breathing increased, her blood roaring in her ears.

When she reached the part of the memory where he'd thrown his head back and growled as he came, her orgasm slammed into her. Her back arched, and she cried out, her hips bucking into her hand as intense pleasure flooded through her.

"Fuck."

Trent's quiet curse came seconds before his mouth settled over hers. His kiss was hard and desperate, his tongue restless in her mouth, demanding a response. When she was pliant and willing and lifting off the sofa to get more of him, he released her and leaned back.

Lauren opened her eyes. Trent knelt beside the sofa, his eyes heavy-lidded and burning through her, breaths as harsh and erratic as her own. The silent acknowledgment moved between them, and she nodded. He gripped her hands and tugged her to her feet, moving down the hallway to his bedroom with long determined strides.

He halted at the foot of his bed and gripped her face in his hands, his mouth coming down on hers, hot and hungry. For a brief moment it became all about that luscious tangle of lips and tongues. Lauren wrapped her arms around his neck, pressing herself as close as she could and rubbing her nipples against his chest for the sweet friction.

Just as suddenly as he'd kissed her, Trent released her. He reached back over his shoulder and yanked off his T-shirt, dropping it to the floor at his feet. She helped him out of his jeans, unbuttoning and unzipping them, then sinking into a crouch as she pulled them down his legs.

He stepped out of them, leaving them wadded on the floor,

and pulled her onto the bed with him. He stared at her as she lay on his chest, eyes full of fire. "Straddle me."

His hoarse demand sent a wave of heat straight through her. She nodded, braced her hands on his chest, and pushed upright. Thighs on either side of him now, her core settled over the length of his erection as she sat back on his hips.

"Just like this." His large, warm hands slid up her thighs to cup her ass, his hips rocking beneath her, showing her what he wanted. His thick erection slid along her slippery cleft, nudging her now-super-sensitive clit.

Lauren moaned, her eyes closing. Her thighs trembled as pleasure erupted through her. "Oh God, that's good."

Trent swore under his breath, his fingers digging into her hips as he set a hard and fast rhythm. She thrust against him in turn, grinding and sliding along his length. The sounds of their pleasure filled the room. His harsh breathing. The quiet moans she couldn't have contained if she tried. Their bodies surged together, pushing against each other, desperate for relief from the fire they'd created in each other.

Another orgasm exploded over her, and Lauren gasped, shaking and jerking as the luscious spasms took her. Beneath her Trent stiffened, thrust against her one last time, then held her firmly in place and groaned from deep within his chest.

She collapsed on top of him. Every limb shook, this time from exhaustion and satiation. Their harsh, erratic breathing filled the otherwise silent room, chests heaving as each attempted to drag in much-needed oxygen. Lauren pressed her face into his neck, immersed herself in his scent, and let it wash over her. Trent banded his arms around her back and turned his head, pressing his cheek to hers.

How long they lay that way, she didn't know, but neither moved. Lauren couldn't find the will. A connection spawned between them in that moment she couldn't deny or ignore. He held her too tightly, and she had no desire to put any distance between them. The longer she lay there, the more the realization settled over her.

"I don't want to wait." She murmured the words into his neck but couldn't bring herself to look at him. If he denied her, she couldn't bear to see the regret fill his eyes. "If all I have is two more weeks with you like this, I want it all. I want to spend every night making love to you, and I want to wake up beside you every morning. No more slow. No more waiting. If we're going to continue this, we need to go all out or it needs to end here."

She squeezed her eyes shut, her heart thudding in painful anticipation of his denial. His excuse. His half-hearted reasons why he needed distance. She was falling in love with him, and she couldn't do it anymore. If she was losing her heart to him, she wanted all of him in return. When the two weeks were over, she'd let him go.

"Agreed." He turned his head, pressing a kiss to her shoulder. "Your place or mine?"

Lauren lifted her head. She hadn't expected him to say that.

He gave her a gentle smile, his hands caressing her back. "I can't deny I want the same thing, but the rest of the deal still stands. In two weeks this ends." His hands stilled on her back, his expression solemn. "I won't lose you."

She stroked his cheek, enjoying the soft scrape of his stubble against her fingertips. "Who says you will?"

Her heart swelled and ached at the same time. The thought of going back to being just a friend to him made her sick to her stomach. Beyond a shadow of a doubt it would break her heart. Who'd have thought it? Her first love would be a man she'd known for most of her life. A man she'd have to continue to see.

She'd just have to deal with it, though. She wasn't stupid enough to think he could love her back. He'd just told her as much.

Neither could she regret spending this time with him. She'd treasure it.

Trent blinked at her for a moment before his expression went carefully impassive. He lay silent. She didn't have to ask to know he'd drawn into himself, that he likely wouldn't tell her what he was thinking, and like every other time, it created distance between them. It had never bothered her before, because it had always been about the war. The memories that haunted him. This time it seemed to be a reaction to their conversation. After everything they'd just shared, it became a side of him she couldn't reach.

He confirmed the thought when he diverted his gaze, his fingers busy stroking her skin. The curve of her ear. Along her jawline.

"I'm bound to disappoint you, Lauren. It's better for both of us if this stays short-lived. I'm not sure I could handle it if you hated me when this was over."

She drew a breath and released it. "Going back to being just friends won't be easy, Trent. I'm not sure I'll be able to turn all of this off just because you want me to."

His fingers stilled and his gaze jerked to hers, eyes widened slightly. As if what she'd said hadn't ever occurred to him. "Would you rather end this now?"

She had to be honest with him here, too. "No. I'm not sorry for this. When I signed up with Military Match, I wanted to lose my virginity to a nice guy. Someone who'd make it something I'd remember with fondness. And that's you."

The tension in his body drained, relief washing across his features. His hands caressed her back again, soft, soothing. "I think you're wrong. We were friends before this. We'll be friends after. That was the whole idea."

She sincerely hoped he was right.

"As for where we do this…" She glanced down, tracing her fingers along his bottom lip. "Where would you be more comfortable? My place or yours?"

"Yours. I hate this apartment." His fingers resumed their torment of her skin, skimming her spine, leaving tingles in his wake. A sudden smile bloomed in his face. "How 'bout we go out tonight?"

She drew her brows together. He'd rarely left his apartment since he'd come home unless it was to go to work. She was pretty sure their first date was *his* first social outing. "Out where?"

One shoulder hitched, his eyes following his fingers as he reached up to tuck her hair back out of her face. "A bar? Club maybe? I don't know. Something fun."

She pursed her lips, worry tightening her stomach. "Can you handle a place like that? It'll be noisy and crowded…"

He let out a sardonic laugh. "I haven't a clue. I'll probably get overwhelmed. But I promised myself when I came home that I'd do everything they couldn't." He turned his head, peering across the room in the direction of his closet. "AJ would've turned twenty-one this month."

Her heart clenched for the grief he clearly hadn't let go of yet. She stroked her fingers over his chest, offering him what she hoped was a pleasant smile. "Then we should go have a drink in his honor."

His gaze returned to her, warmth and something that looked a lot like relief shining in his eyes. "Exactly. I'm hoping you being there will help."

She brushed her mouth over his. "I shall do my best to keep you distracted, then."

* * *

As it turned out, Lauren kept her promise. They ended up in a jazz club. The place hosted a local live band every night, and you could order food and drinks while you watched them play. Okay, so he preferred eighties hard rock, but while the place was full, the space didn't give him the sensation of being closed in. The music wasn't thundering through his head or setting off a flashback, but was mellow and soothing.

Seated in a booth at the back of the club, Trent was nursing a beer. Lauren had chosen some fruity, icy mix. Being here amazed him. He hadn't been in a bar since before he'd come home. Or hell, a restaurant for that matter. Normally, he couldn't handle crowded, noisy spaces. Tonight, though, Lauren's presence beside him soothed whatever raw nerves he might have had.

She turned to smile at him, a soft, self-pleased light in her eyes. "You're enjoying yourself."

"I actually am." So much so he couldn't wait to get her home. When he'd agree to their new arrangement, he'd had all kinds of lofty plans. He'd make her wait until tomorrow night, and he'd do it right. Take his time. Seduce her with wine and dinner. Hell, she deserved it. And more.

Now? Now he ached to feel her supple skin against his. To bury himself inside of her and make her a part of him. She was right. If all they had was another two weeks, he wanted as much of her as he could get. He wanted to make love to her until they were exhausted and spent. Then fall asleep wrapped around her. Since their conversation earlier, he couldn't stop thinking about what she'd said. He'd pondered continuing what they had only to come to the same conclusion. The thought of losing her still scared the crap out of him. Eventually he'd push her beyond her tolerance. He'd fail her, the way he had AJ and Cooper and, hell, even Wendy. And then she'd hate him.

He ought to be letting her go. Let her find someone else who could give her everything he couldn't. Continuing even for the next two weeks was selfish and he damn well knew it. But he couldn't make himself end it.

He wanted this time with her. Memories to take with him when it ended, to keep him warm in the dark loneliness of night. But he had no desire to wait until tomorrow to make love to her.

He blindly groped for her hand, threading their fingers once he found it, and leaned his mouth beside her ear so she'd hear him over the music, and because he meant the words only for her. He prayed she understood. "Tonight."

She nodded, shivering against his side. Her eyes drooped to half-mast, burning through him. She shifted their combined hands, sliding hers over his thigh beneath the table and inching upward. In two seconds flat, he was hard, his cock swelling and thickening behind his zipper.

He halted the movement of her hand before she managed to reach her destination, and shook his head, then turned back to the band. She made him feel...human. Normal. She'd taken him places he didn't think he could have gotten to on his own. And he wanted to hold on to it for just a while longer.

They spent the next hour sipping drinks and sharing a basket of fries. Needing the physical connection, he kept hold of one of her hands, idly stroking the delicate inner skin of her wrist. Her awareness of him prickled in the air between them, creating a delicious but relaxed tension.

When the band took a small break, Lauren leaned toward him, her warm breath whispering over his cheek. "Time to go home."

The husky tone of her voice had his cock swelling to life all over again. He nodded, because he couldn't have refused if he tried.

She stood, pulling him up with her, and he took a moment to drop a tip for the waitress on the table before letting Lauren pull him outside. They'd agreed before leaving to take a cab home. Waiting on the cool, darkened Seattle street, he stood behind her, arms wrapped around her. She leaned her head back on his shoulder, but her hands were restless, sliding up and down his thighs.

The cab ride itself had to be the most torturous drive he'd ever endured and seemed to take forever. They rode in unbearable silence, the tension prickling in the air between them. Antsy with anticipation, he couldn't keep his knee from bouncing. His erection pressed painfully against his zipper, and he couldn't do a damn thing about it because they weren't alone.

Lauren seemed to enjoy his torture. One glance at her had him swallowing a groan. Mischief and amusement danced in those gorgeous eyes, mixing with a heat that only added fuel to the blaze in his belly. "Restless?"

The minx.

He rolled his eyes, but damned if he could stop his smile all the same. "You're enjoying my torture far too much, doll."

She squeezed his thigh. "Going out *was* your idea."

He shot her a sideways glare, resisting the nearly overwhelming urge to take that hand burning through his jeans and curl it around him just to ease the ache. "So it was."

Twenty minutes later, the cab finally stopped in front of her house. Lauren released his knee and climbed from the car. Trent took a moment to pull his wallet from his back pocket. He got out two twenties and tossed them at the driver, but didn't wait for change.

By the time he'd jogged up the front walk and made it onto the porch, Lauren had the front door unlocked and was pushing it open. Striding up behind her, he grabbed her around the waist, sweeping her inside and shoving the door closed with his foot.

She squealed, then let out a giggle that made his heart pound with a giddy sense of euphoria. He was already shaking, his desire so keen he wasn't sure he'd actually make it to the sex.

Fuck. It had been too damn long since he'd felt this... free. And it was all her fault.

He yanked her against him and sealed his mouth over hers. Her happy giggling became a quiet moan that set his blood on fire. Lauren plastered her lithe body against his, pushing her breasts into his chest, and reached down. When she popped the button free on his jeans, he groaned into her mouth.

The energy between them exploded. Piece by piece, clothing got ripped off and tossed aside, littering the floor as they made their way to the bedroom. He lost his shirt on their way past the sofa. She lost her bra outside the hallway bathroom. His jeans made it all the way to the bedroom doorway before she sank to her knees and yanked them down.

Once over the threshold to the room, she released his mouth

and backed away enough to peel her panties off—a lovely red satin pair. After stepping out of them, she pressed along his length and claimed his mouth again. She was beautiful like this, sure of herself, taking what she wanted. Just that much, the luscious slide of her warm, satiny skin against his, nearly made him lose what little control he had.

It didn't help that her hands were doing exactly what his were—roaming. Over his chest. Down his abdomen. She slipped them beneath the waistband of his shorts, pushing them down his thighs. The fabric barely hit the floor before she was wrapping herself around him again.

Another groan ripped out of him. God, she felt good. Her taut nipples rubbed his chest with her every subtle movement. Her hands were warm, her skin smooth and creamy. His aching erection became caught against the softness of her belly. It was all he could do not to grab her waist and rub himself all over her, for the glorious freedom of his cock sliding against her warm, satiny skin.

He needed to be inside her more, though, and tumbled her to the bed, settling himself over her. Her quiet demand this afternoon had cracked his shell. He needed this. To feel her body beneath him and to bury himself so damn deep inside her he might never see the light of day again.

What he needed the most…was to be a part of her and, in turn, to make her a part of him. The intensity of that need scared the living shit out of him, but he couldn't deny it either.

All sense of play faded as he settled between her thighs. Lauren stared up at him, her body trembling beneath him, big brown eyes liquid and tender. He stroked the hair back off her face, enjoying the simplicity of its softness sifting through his fingers. He needed to take this slow. Lauren was a virgin, and if he sank deep, he'd hurt her.

She slid her hands up his back, thighs bending to cradle his hips. "You're shaking."

"Because I need you." He brushed a kiss across her mouth and moved off her long enough to retrieve the condom from his pants pocket. After putting it on, he settled himself over her again. His nerves got the best of him then. His stomach twisted. "There's no easy way about this, doll."

"Then don't think about it." Lauren claimed his mouth, slid her hands down his back to his cup his ass, and arched against him. He slid home in one slick, deliciously slow thrust, her body wrapping around him like a warm, wet glove.

Lauren winced and squeezed her eyes shut, trembling beneath him for all the wrong reasons. A sick sensation rolled through his stomach. Fuck he hated this. Sex wasn't supposed to cause pain. Damn it.

"I'm sorry. I promise it'll get better from here on out." Desperate to make up for hurting her, he rained kisses over her cheeks, her nose, her mouth. "Open your eyes, doll. Look at me."

She did as he asked, but instead of tenderness or need, her eyes searched his in apprehension.

So as he moved slowly within her, he leaned on an elbow, using one hand to caress any part of her he could reach. Down her side and over her hip. Her breast and nipple. All the while watching her eyes and hoping his touches would slowly ease her anxiety.

"Touch me." He brushed a tender kiss across her mouth. "Forget the pain and touch me."

Her eyes searched his, still full of too much nervousness, body still a little too stiff beneath him. "Where?"

"Wherever you want." He sipped at her mouth, determined to make that fear—because that's exactly what it was—leave her eyes. "Nothing's changed. It's still just me. Focus on me."

She nodded, her hands finally beginning to move over him. Up his back to his shoulders. Back down to cup his ass. The more she touched, the more she relaxed beneath him.

"That's it." Every muscle in his body tensed with the effort it took to go slow. She was so hot and so fucking tight. If he moved any quicker, he wouldn't last. He reached down and pulled one leg over his hip, changing the angle and easing in deeper. "Move with me."

Lauren nodded and rolled her hips, thrusting against him. Her pelvis glided against his, and she moaned, this one full of pleasure. Her eyes rolled back and closed. "Oh, that's nice."

He let out a breathless laugh. His ego wanted "phenomenal" and "unbelievable" and "sex God," but that one small sound was a salve on his soul. The knots in his shoulders finally unraveled. That sound meant she'd begun to enjoy herself.

So he bent his head to her neck, suckling any part of her he could reach. "Want to know what you feel like for me?"

He rocked against her, pushing in deeper, and she moaned again, this one tortured and full of sweet agony. "Y-yes."

"Hot. You're hot, doll. And so fucking tight." Another thrust as they rocked against each other pulled a deep groan out of him. A ripple of pleasure moved through him, and his control slipped another notch. "You feel incredible."

Slowly but surely she relaxed, no longer nervous but rising to meet him with an ever-increasing tempo. With every thrust, she urged him on with soft moans of *"Oh God"* and *"Sooo good."*

"Fuck." He dropped his head into the crook of her shoulder,

losing himself in…her. Her soft scent, her body beneath him, around him. Her pleasure was the ultimate turn-on. Every sigh and moan only ramped up the need burning through him like wildfire. Like he was a kid all over again, with no ability to control himself.

No. If he was going, he was taking her with him.

He rolled onto his back, pulling her on top of him, and pushed her legs flat. Then he slid his hands to her ass, gripping her tight, and thrust up into her, showing her what he wanted. This position would be better for her.

"Circles, doll." He lifted his head, nipped, licked, and kissed her neck, her shoulders, her jaw. "Roll your hips. Grind against me."

He showed her a few times what he meant, causing her clit to rub his pelvis and him to slide inside her in slow, delicious increments. She went limp on top of him, dropped her forehead onto his shoulder, and moaned into his throat.

He turned his head, murmuring into her hair, "Let it go. Come with me, Lauren. Come with me."

The moan she let out next sounded torn from deep within her and filled his whole being until there was nothing but her. With every thrust, she rolled her hips, panting and mewling into his throat, and with every one, he pushed deeper, moving faster. The need to somehow fuse with her pounded around inside his chest.

She let out a quiet, indrawn gasp, and her hips gained a jerky rhythm, her inner muscles clamping around him with the start of her orgasm. Trent lost his hold on what little self-control he'd ever had and came, blinding and hot. All he could do was hold on to her as she took his careful world and spun it beyond his imagination.

When the spasms ended, Lauren dropped onto his chest, body limp, breathing as jagged as his. She slid her hands beneath him, hugging him hard, and pressed her face into his neck.

"Don't let go." Her voice came as a bare murmur into his throat, filled with a vulnerability that pulled at the deepest part of him. "Please don't let go. Not yet."

"I won't." Trent wrapped his arms around her in turn and hugged her just as hard, his chest aching. How the hell could he ever let her go after this?

CHAPTER THIRTEEN

Lauren woke several hours later to soft lips nuzzling her earlobe and a large, calloused palm sliding into the curls between her thighs. Trent lay against her side, his skin lusciously warm. His erection lay hot and hard against her hip, and just that fast, moisture gathered between her thighs. She didn't bother to open her eyes but moaned softly and reached out blindly to touch him. Upon finding his soft belly, she caressed down, curling her fingers around his length, and stroked him gently.

He groaned low in his throat and nipped at her shoulder. "Are you sore?"

The husky rumble of his voice sent a wave of heat bursting along her skin. Despite his question, his deft fingers caressed her, sliding over sensitive skin. When the tip of his finger caressed her clit, fire erupted through her. She *was* a bit sore, as she'd been told she might be after her first time. She'd secretly hoped Trent would be right, that she'd be so turned on it wouldn't hurt the first time. When it had, she'd become overwhelmed. Feeling pain in a moment that was supposed to be all about pleasure had left her floundering. Uncertain.

Trent had calmed it all. So despite her soreness, she couldn't resist the need he sent burning through her.

She slid her hand over his, pressing him more firmly into her. "Don't stop."

He groaned low in her ear, his lips moving over her. Skimming her jaw. Nipping at her shoulder. Sending showers of sparks erupting over the surface of her skin.

"I wanted to let you sleep, thought you might be too sore, but…" He arched his hips, his impressive length sliding against her palm, and groaned again. "God, I want you."

She stroked him slowly, all the while rocking her hips into his hand. "I am, but…" His fingers caressed her again, and the rest of her sentence died on a strangled gasp.

One touch and every nerve ending came alive as he swept her up in a world of sensation: the huff of his erratic breathing in her ear, his long fingers buried inside of her, stroking all the right places, building the need to breathtaking heights. Faster than she thought possible, her orgasm burst through her, luxurious and bone-melting.

When the spasms finally slowed to aftershocks, she gave a luxurious stretch and rolled toward him. He was little more than a shadow in the darkness, but that intense gaze burned into her.

He slid a warm palm over the curve of her hip, gripped her ass, and rocked his erection into the softness of her belly. Then he groaned, this time a sound of misery and need, and caught her bottom lip between his teeth. "Condom."

She nodded, brushed a kiss over his mouth, and rolled away from him, fumbling in the top drawer of her nightstand. Fingers closing around a foil packet, she rolled back to him and held out the condom. "I haven't a clue what I'm doing, and I don't want to wait for lessons…"

He grinned in the darkness and took the condom, quickly putting it on, then hooked her knee and pulled her leg over his hip. Once again his large, warm palm cupped her ass, pulling her to him as he arched upward, sliding deep inside her in one slow, slick thrust.

This time they both moaned, and he leaned his forehead against hers. "If I'm too rough…"

She pressed her leg into his buttocks, pulling him hard to her, and arched tightly against him.

"I'm not afraid, Trent." She tilted her head, brushing kisses over his mouth. "Let go. I want you to let go."

He claimed her mouth in a hard kiss and used his purchase on her ass to set the rhythm. She wrapped both arms around him and met his every thrust by pushing against him. How was it possible to need someone like this? Their lovemaking took on a desperate rhythm, bodies surging together, and every thrust lit her body on fire. Every nerve ending came alive all over again until she was panting and making sounds she didn't know she *could* make. Desperate, pleasure-filled moans and sighs.

It wasn't long before that sweet bubble burst inside of her again, and she was shuddering in his arms. Trent groaned low in her ear, following quickly, his body trembling against her as he came.

He let out his breath in a rush and dropped his forehead into her neck, his arm tightening around her. They lay that way for a moment, just their harsh breathing filling the silence. Finally he lifted his head, kissed her softly, and pulled away from her. "I'll be right back."

He left the room naked, returning a few minutes later, climbed in beside her, and drew her to him. She rested her head on his chest and he wrapped his arms around her, holding her so tight she couldn't sure be where he ended and she began.

* * *

A week later she woke to bright sunlight pervading the room. Signs of life drifted in from outside. Kids laughing. Dogs barking. Cars starting.

Lauren opened her eyes to find Trent on his side, hand tucked beneath his pillow, watching her. The intensity in those cobalt eyes told her something heavy weighed on his mind, but he smiled all the same, soft and warm, and pressed a gentle kiss to her lips. "Morning."

"Morning." She returned the smile, trying to pretend her heart didn't clench.

She couldn't have asked for a more perfect first time. Despite his making her promise to tell him if he got too rough, he'd been everything she'd always envisioned a man would be: tender, gentle, considerate. God, he had passion, too. Now she knew why he didn't do one-night stands any more than she did. Because when he made love, he didn't hold back. She didn't get bits and parts of him. She got all of him.

She reached back into the nightstand drawer for a condom, then rolled him onto his back and straddled his hips. "I want you."

Big warm hands skimmed her body, his breaths already coming hard and fast. He let out a quiet laugh. "I'm not sure I'll ever get enough of you."

Her heart swelled and ached at his tender admission. Their time together was slowly dwindling. They hadn't talked about it.

Rather, they seemed to be ignoring it completely. But it was there between them all the same, like a thick black cloud hanging over their heads.

"Me either." She grinned at him as she slid down his body. Her trembling fingers fumbled to roll the condom down his length. Then she straddled him again and sank onto him, taking him inch by glorious inch. Yeah. This feeling. Him inside of her, body meshed with hers. She wasn't sure she'd ever get enough of it, either.

"Closer." He pulled her down to lie on him, chest to chest.

They made love slowly, rocking together, arms banded around each other, sharing the same breath. Never once did he look away, and she lost herself there, in the deep blue sea of his eyes. She was drowning in him, but she had no desire to be saved. He took her world and spun it beyond her imagination. Until there was nothing but him and the glorious pleasure he sent spiraling through her.

He rose to meet her as she sank down, and with every luscious thrust, the rhythm increased. Until they were pushing and shoving together. She couldn't seem to take him deep enough, and the sounds of their frantic lovemaking filled the room, their bodies slapping together, the bed creaking. Her soft pants combined with his harsh breaths.

Her orgasm struck out of nowhere, luxurious and soft, but powerful all the same. Her eyes fluttered closed as the bliss racked her body. "Trent…"

He let out a deep groan, his hands gripping her ass tight to hold her still as he shook beneath her.

She collapsed on his chest, still trembling, and pressed her face into his neck, his scent filling her nostrils with every gasping breath. Trent kissed her head and held her tightly, but neither of them spoke.

When her breathing finally slowed, she shifted off him and sat up. Trent lay there for a minute before he rose from the bed. He touched her shoulder, then left the room, striding down the hallway. The bathroom door shut with a resounding click. Or maybe it was just her.

She was too aware that their time together was dwindling fast. She had one more week with him this way. When it was over, Trent would set her back in the friend zone, and she'd have to pretend seeing him didn't make her heart ache. Didn't make her want more with him or doubt herself as a woman. Once again, she'd be rejected and alone, and she had to pretend it wasn't killing her. After all, she'd agreed to this. Could she even go back to treating him like only a friend?

One thing became clear as the finest crystal: she really wasn't cut out for flings.

* * *

Later that week, Lauren stood at the stove, trying to keep her mind focused on her task. Namely, making breakfast. She pulled the spatula through the scrambled eggs in the pan, one ear on the water running at the back of the house. Trent was in the shower. He'd come out soon dressed in just his jeans and greet her with a tender kiss on his way to the coffeemaker. Like he always did.

All the while she'd have to pretend her chest wasn't caving in.

The date had leaped out at her from her phone when she'd checked her voice mail twenty minutes ago. Their month had come to an end. For the past two weeks, Trent had taken to staying at her place. She went to sleep every night with his warm, solid body wrapped against her back after making love to him until she was too sated to move. She woke every morning to his stubbled face and bright eyes.

But now all that was over, because it was what they'd agreed on.

Tomorrow morning her life would go back to normal. Whatever the hell that was these days. A week from now they had Will and Skylar's party. She'd have to go back to treating Trent like a friend.

The ache in her chest told her one thing in no uncertain terms: she'd gone and done exactly what she shouldn't have. She'd fallen in love with him. She couldn't even be sure when it happened. She only knew the thought of never again getting to touch him, or kiss him, or fall asleep wrapped in his arms was crushing her.

The water shut off, leaving her alone with her twisting thoughts. By the time the eggs were done, he emerged around the corner in nothing but a pair of worn jeans, chest deliciously bare.

Lauren focused on divvying out the eggs. If she didn't, she'd be pushing herself into his arms, which would get her all of nowhere. The time had come to separate herself from this. The problem was, she hadn't a damn clue how to do that.

Trent sidled up behind her, settling his hands on her waist. "Tell me."

Of course he knew something was off. Like she was made of freaking glass.

She shook her head, attempting to step out of his embrace. "It's nothing. I'm fine."

Trent slid his arms around her, pulling her flush against him. His voice came as a husky rumble against her back. "You're not fine. I know your every mood, and I know when something's wrong. Spill it."

They'd promised each other honesty, but what the hell could she tell him? How did she do this?

She sighed, tears pricking at her eyes. She'd hoped they wouldn't have to have this conversation yet, but sooner or later she had to face it. "Today's our last day together."

He didn't say anything for a moment, but his body stiffened against her back.

"That's what I thought it was." He released her and stepped away, moving around her to the coffeemaker. "It's what we agreed on. A month and it ends."

His voice was low, devoid of any emotion that might clue her in to how he felt.

She nodded and moved to the bread she'd set on the counter earlier, pulling out two pieces and popping them into the toaster. "Yup. We did."

"So what's the problem?" Spoken with little emotion. Like they merely discussed whether to go out tonight.

She gripped the counter's edge until her fingertips hurt. The words burned like acid on her tongue, but she'd spent the last twenty minutes in contemplation, and her thoughts swirled like buzzards over a dead carcass, continually returning to one point. She couldn't do this with him anymore. "I was thinking maybe we should just end this now instead of tomorrow morning."

Having poured hot coffee into a mug, Trent returned the carafe to the base and stood silent. Tension rose over him, thickening the air between them. Finally, his facade cracked and he pivoted toward her, brows draw together, blue eyes filled with…misery. With regret. "Lauren…"

Her insides wobbled. She took a step back and shook her head.

"Don't. If you care about me at all, Trent, you won't tell me what I know you're going to. I know what this is and what it isn't."

His jaw tightened. His nostrils flared. Fists clenched at his sides. For a moment he stared, clearly at war with himself. Then he drew a deep breath and released it, his fists unfurling. "What's changed, then?"

"Me." She let out a harsh, bitter laugh and turned to the stove, for something, anything else to look at but the regret in his eyes. "Apparently, I'm no good at flings. I know we agreed on this, but I can't pretend this isn't killing me. I'm sorry, but I'm human. And I don't want to spend the day dreading that moment when I have to watch you leave and not come back. I'd rather we just get it over with now. Go our separate ways."

While she still had the strength not to beg him to stay.

She stared at his back, waiting for him to say…something.

Finally, he pivoted toward her, slid a hand around her waist, and hauled her against him. His eyes blazed, nostrils flaring. "We have one more night, and I want it."

"What does one more night matter?" It would only hurt worse tomorrow when she had to wake in his arms again.

Trent didn't answer, but cupped her face in his palms and sealed his mouth over hers. His kiss wasn't the soft, tender sips and tastes she'd come to know, either. His lips bruised hers, his tongue thrusting inside, demanding a response. God help her, she gave him one. She arched her back, pushing her breasts into his chest, and lifted onto her toes to get more of him.

He was a drug, and she was addicted. A fly willingly caught in his web.

As if sensing her surrender, he turned her back to the counter. His large, warm hands furrowed beneath the waistband of her pajama pants and pushed them down. When they pooled at her feet, he gripped her now bare ass in his hands and lifted her like she weighed nothing, setting her down on the counter, then edged between her thighs. He reclaimed her lips, never once giving her room to protest, as his hands moved to his fly, unbuttoning and unzipping his jeans. He released her long enough to shove them down his hips, then pulled her to him and thrust home.

Lauren gasped at the sweet invasion, her body arching into his. She couldn't say no to him any more than she could stop breathing. Her body rose to his, her hips thrusting against him.

He wasn't gentle or tender or slow. His hips pumped into her, his rhythm hard and fast and brutal. His thick length filled her insides, sliding so deep it bordered on the brink of pain. And yet she couldn't stop herself from responding. He hit a sweet spot deep inside, and pleasure erupted along her nerve endings. Her body liquefied, his to do with as he pleased.

He thrust deep again and again, and Lauren wrapped her arms around his shoulders, holding tight. She pushed against him, welcoming the luscious tension coiling within her, her last chance to connect to him.

Trent dropped his head onto her shoulder, never once apologizing or slowing, but continually pushing harder, deeper, beyond her boundaries…then demanding more.

It didn't last long. In a matter of minutes they were shuddering together, her body bowing into him, shaking uncontrollably as her orgasm claimed her. He groaned into her throat, his hips jerking as he emptied himself deep inside of her.

Just as quickly as it began, it ended, leaving her shaking, a sense of ultra-vulnerability curling through her. "I want more, Trent."

She wanted to keep what they had. Even if there was a chance they wouldn't last. Even it was only a few months. She wanted all of him. Wanted to call him her boyfriend, to announce their relationship to the whole damn world.

Wanted him to tell her he wanted her, too.

His body stiffened against her. He held her for the briefest seconds, then pulled out and turned away from her, doing up his pants as he left the room.

Her chest squeezed, all the air leaving her lungs. His seed already spilled out to coat her inner thighs, no doubt making a mess of her kitchen counter. Never mind that they hadn't even thought about a condom or the fact that she could end up pregnant. Wouldn't that just be cat's meow? Having his baby knowing he didn't love her. The thought was killing her, and she couldn't move. She sat frozen, afraid if she so much as breathed, she'd shatter into a thousand, irreparable shards.

A minute later Trent stopped in the kitchen entrance, fully dressed now. His brow furrowed, eyes filled with a palpable regret. "I'm sorry, Lauren. I am. But I can't."

He didn't wait for her to respond, but turned and strode away. The entire house seemed to fill with an unbearable strained silence that gripped her chest in a vise.

Thirty seconds later the front door opened with a whoosh of air disturbed, then closed with a quiet snap. She flinched and held her breath, knowing what was coming but waiting for it all the same. When his motorcycle growled to life outside in the driveway, the tears finally came. As she listened to his engine fading into the distance, they dripped one by one down her cheeks.

It was over. She loved him, and he wasn't coming back. The sad part was, as much as it hurt, she couldn't be sorry for the time she'd spent with him. He'd given her something she could never in a million years regret: all of himself. For a single, glorious month, he was hers. He'd taught her that sex wasn't the evil thing she'd grown up believing it to be. It could be beautiful and life altering. He'd calmed her insecurities and proven it really was possible that a good man could want her.

He'd given her wings, freedom from the past. Freedom to revel in her sexuality, to glorify in it even.

She'd also accomplished what she'd set out to do when she'd signed up for that blasted dating service. She'd lost her virginity. She'd had her first fling and, now, her first love. All in one fell swoop. She'd treasure those memories. Even if right now all they did was make her want to curl into a ball on the floor and sob.

* * *

He was miserable. He was at a party meant to be a celebration, a night of fun, and he was fucking miserable.

Seated on the steps of the back deck of his parents' house a week later, Trent braced his elbows on his knees and stared out over the darkened yard. There were no less than a hundred people milling about the space, half of whom he'd never met. The sun had long since set, and three hours in, the party was still going strong. They'd set up tables outside, and Dad had brought out the tiki torches, setting a glowing perimeter around the yard.

Mom had done exactly what he'd expected. She'd insisted on cooking, and now moved from table to table playing the ultimate hostess, checking on her guests and refilling plates and drinks. Will and Sky were ensconced in the middle of a crowd, laughing and talking. Dad, last he'd checked, was telling war stories.

The whole evening was a huge success. Everyone appeared to be having fun. Everyone except him.

He'd put on cheerful facade, for his brother's sake, had made a toast in their honor, had laughed and forced himself to mingle. Now he had a damn headache. He couldn't get into the mood if he tried.

Skylar had, of course, invited Lauren. Mom had roped her into bringing dessert. She now stood at the makeshift buffet table, helping his mother refill drinks or plates. She looked incredible, in a simple pair of black slacks and a soft sweater that outlined her curves, her hair spilling free down her back and blowing in the cool evening breeze. She was on top of her game, too, gracious as always, laughing and talking.

She hadn't said a word to him since she'd arrived four hours ago. She wouldn't even look at him. Every once in a while she'd glance in his direction, but longing and hurt would fleet through her gaze... right before it skirted off in another direction.

And it was eating a hole in his chest. It was ironic, really. The whole damn idea of his stupid rules and the one-month time limit had been to keep it casual, to keep her from getting hurt, so that in the end he wouldn't lose her. Yet here he was. He'd lost her anyway.

What a fool he'd been.

Will turned his head, his gaze landing on Trent for a moment. Then he turned to Skylar and leaned in to her ear. Skylar nodded, and Will stepped away from the crowd.

Trent's gut tightened as he watched Will move in his direction. So much for being inconspicuous.

After climbing the steps, Will dropped neat and easy beside him. "Only you could look miserable at a party."

"Sorry. I figured you and Sky would be wrapped up in each other by now and nobody would miss me." Trent shot his brother an apologetic frown, then turned his gaze back to the yard.

"We'll always miss you." Will bumped his shoulder. "I couldn't help noticing that you've been watching Lauren all night. How come you're up here looking miserable instead of down there with her? You haven't said two words to each other all night. What happened?"

He eyed Lauren, who now sat at a table between Mandy and some big buff dude. As he watched, the dude leaned toward her, apparently saying something funny, because Lauren turned her head and laughed, her whole face lighting up.

Irritation slid along his nerve endings, and Trent's jaw tightened. Along with his stomach. Only sheer force of will kept him in his seat. What he wanted to do was march the hell down there.

Will nudged him with an elbow. "Relax. That's Chris, Sky's brother-in-law. He's happily married."

Trent blew out a breath, releasing his irritation along with it. Christ. He was acting like a jealous ex. From now on it would be this way. Chances were he wouldn't see much of her, save for holidays or the summer barbeques his parents like to throw, but he'd have to prepare himself for the eventuality of it. Along with the eventuality of her dating again. He'd have to watch her be with someone else and pretend it didn't make him see red.

This whole fiasco had been *his* brilliant fucking idea.

He dropped his head into his hands, dejection weighing on him. "It was a fling and it's over. We agreed on short-lived, that we'd go back to being friends when it ended. Problem is, she hasn't said two words to me in more than a week. She won't even look at me."

"Ah." Will nodded as if he'd suddenly figured it all out and turned to stare at the yard for a moment. "You want my advice?"

Trent let out a sardonic laugh. "Do I have a choice?"

"No." Will shot him a cockeyed grin and pushed to his feet. "Forgive me for being blunt, bro, but stop being a stubborn ass and just admit you're in love with her. Then for crying out loud, go down there and tell *her.* I know you're afraid of losing of her, but if you ask me, it would seem you already have. So what the hell have you got to lose?" Will nudged him with his knee. "Time to pick up and move on, T. I can't think of anyone more perfect for you than her."

Will didn't bother to wait for a response, but trotted down the steps into the yard, leaving Trent to stare after him. His pulse pounded in his ears as Will's words repeated in his head. *Just admit you're in love with her.*

Reality slanted sideways, then slammed him against the wall. Hell. *Was* he in love with her?

Right behind the realization came the sinking pain. Did it even matter? Could he be anything she needed?

* * *

Trent punched Lauren's doorbell, then pivoted and turned to pace the length of the porch. Three steps to the left. About-face. Three steps to the right. Wash, rinse, and repeat. It was two in the freakin' morning. Lauren was no doubt sleeping, but damned if he could sleep. He'd lain in bed pondering his brother's words for hours now.

Until finally they'd driven him nuts and he'd gotten out of bed. He wasn't even sure why he was here, except that he'd come to the same conclusion Will had. What the hell did he have to lose at this point? She needed to know she meant more to him than just a month of great sex.

The dead bolt gave a noisy *thunk* behind him. Every muscle tightened, binding into a tight little ball that sat, hard and heavy, in his stomach. His nerve endings were on edge, raw, waiting for her to open that door.

When she finally did, his restless nerves ground to a halt. Whatever the hell it was he'd planned to say flew right out of his head. Lauren stood on the other side of the threshold, worry creasing her forehead, wearing those worn pajamas and a clingy white tank top.

"Trent." Her eyes widened in surprise, then just as quickly her expression blanked. The walls went up over her, like someone had drawn the shades, and she folded her arms, dropping her gaze to her feet as she flexed her bare toes against the floor. "It's late. Are you okay?"

His gut knotted, regret twisting through his chest. Of course she'd ask him that. She ought to hate him, but deep down where it counted, she still cared.

God, he was such a fool. He knew now why he'd come.

He wanted her. All of her. Maybe he'd fail. Hell, he'd be lucky if she let him past the door. But he had to try. Because his world didn't make sense without her anymore.

He stepped up to the doorway. Somehow he managed to stop himself from stepping over the threshold and sweeping her into his arms for the desperate need to feel her against him. It had been only a week, but it had felt like an eternity. But if he touched her, it had to be her choice. So he stuffed his hands in his pockets. "No. Can we talk?"

She looked up, misery and exhaustion in her eyes. "I'm tired, Trent. It's been a long night."

"I know, but this can't wait." Too keyed up to wait for permission, he stepped forward, grabbed her hand, and pulled her the beyond the door enough to close it. If he didn't say the words now, he might never get another chance.

He led her into the living room, then released her hand and faced her. One look at those big brown eyes and everything he wanted to tell her got narrowed down to three impossible words.

His shoulders slumped. "I miss you."

Tears flooded her eyes, and Lauren folded her arms again, dropping her gaze to the tan carpeting. "Don't do this to me. It's not fair."

He took that step, closed the distance between them as much as he dared, but stuffed his free hand back in his pocket. "I'm not here to make your life miserable. I just realized something I need you to know."

She lifted her gaze and shook her head, looking at him like he'd lost his mind. "Then say it, so you can leave and I can go back to bed."

His gut roiled, his chest aching. Will was right. Their friendship never would've recovered from this.

He released a heavy breath. "I don't blame you for hating me."

She let out a huff of a laugh. "I don't hate you. I just can't stuff my feelings back into that neat little box you want me to and pretend like I can be just your friend."

Hope blossomed inside of him. Maybe, just maybe, she'd forgive him for being a blind fool.

He drew a breath and launched into the speech he'd been telling her over and over in his head for hours.

"I came home a year and a half ago feeling like a part of me had died. Hell, part of me wished I had. I lived in the dark, went through the motions. But spending time with you?" He shook his head, unable to stop himself from reaching out to her, caressing her chin with his thumb. She shivered beneath his touch, and he only just managed to stop himself from moving closer. "You opened me. Made me live. Hell. You made me *want* to live. You made me feel human again."

He stopped to judge her reaction. Waited for her to say something. When she didn't, when she shifted from one foot to the other and tugged her chin from his grasp, he sighed and went on. She listened at least. That had to count for something.

"Every day since we ended this, I've gone back to living in the dark. My apartment is cold and empty. I finished that carving of you. It's gorgeous. But like all the rest, it sits in the closet because I can't bear to look at it. It reminds me of you. I get up every morning more alone than I did the day before. A piece of me is missing, and it took Will pointing it out to me to realize what it was."

He caught the wobble in her lower lip right before she turned her back to him, staring in the direction of the wall of curtained windows on the other side of the room. Her shoulders were stiff, her back straight. Clearly she didn't intend to make this easy.

So he stepped up behind her, close enough that her sleep-warm skin infused his. A shiver moved through her that had his hands fisting with the effort not to touch, not to invade her space. "Aren't you going to ask me what that something is?"

She shook her head. "I'm not sure what you're trying to prove here, but this is cruel, Trent."

The wobble in her voice sapped the last of his willpower. He pulled his hands from his pockets and slipped his arms around her waist, tugging her back against him. She didn't go willingly, but she didn't pull away, either. It was something, at least. So he continued. "I'm not trying to be. I just need you to know. That something is you."

Her breathing hitched, and his chest tightened. He'd hurt her, and he hated himself for it. All he could do now was pray that somehow, when it was all said and done, she'd understand.

"I've kept you at a distance because I'm terrified to lose you. You're a light in the dark, Lauren. But you wouldn't even look at me tonight. You haven't said two words to me since I left, and it's eating at me. I haven't slept since I left your apartment that morning, you know that? Because I miss you. I miss every damn thing about you. Your smile. The sound of your laugh. Hell, I miss you teasing me. But you know what I miss the most?"

This time he waited. He needed some sort of reaction from her. Encouragement. A *go to hell.* Something to tell him he was getting to her. She listened, but he was even making a dent?

When she continued to remain silent, he leaned his head beside her ear and rushed on. He'd come all the way out here at two in the morning. At the very least, he needed to say the words. "I miss waking up to you in the morning."

Finally, she relented and sagged back into him. It was a movement of submission, and his chest tightened. She was trembling and for all the wrong reasons. "Why are you telling me all this?"

"Because I need you to know"—he tightened his hold on her and ducked his head, pressing his cheek to hers—"I'm in love with you."

Lauren's breathing hitched, and she pulled out of his embrace, stepping away from him. She kept her back to him and wrapped her arms around herself. She wasn't giving him an inch, and who the hell could blame her? But neither had she asked him to leave. That was something. So he drew a breath and kept going.

"I have to be honest with you, though, doll. I don't know how to do this. I've failed at this once already, and the thought of losing you still scares the shit out of me. My marriage went down in a spiral to hell, and I know damn well it takes two to make or break a marriage. I can't blame it all on her."

Lauren finally turned to face him. Tears streaked her cheeks, but her brows furrowed in irritation. "She cheated on you. That trumps whatever problems you might have had."

"I'm not entirely convinced of that. Would she still have left had I been any kind of husband to her? Or were we doomed from the start? I don't think I'll ever know." He dropped his gaze to the floor, the tan carpeting blurring as his gaze went unfocused. "I've got a lot of shit going on inside. Cooper and AJ died because of me, and I don't know how to live with that. I was supposed to protect them. Every night I see them. Those images haunt me. There are days I wake up feeling like I'm still over there."

He finally forced himself to look up at her. Focused on her big brown eyes and hoped, somehow, he was making sense.

"That's what she had to live with. What *you'd* have to deal with. You want to know why I made up all those damn rules? That's it. Because I was positive I'd only make you miserable. Most nights are endless for me. The dreams wake me from a dead sleep. Often, I pace the floors because I'm terrified to close my eyes for fear I'll see it again. I've been home nineteen months now, and it hasn't lessened by much. I've just learned to cope a little better.

"There are days when I'm so ornery I can't stand myself. Because every little sound is a fucking grenade going off beside me, and I'm jumpy as hell. And there are times when being around people is the last thing I want, when all I want is my space, to sort it all out on my own."

He reached out slowly, caressing his fingers along her cheek. She didn't flinch or swat his hand away. That had to be a good thing, right?

"But I'm miserable without you. My world has gone dark again. I get up. I go through the motions. But it's empty. I don't want to go back to living like that. I want you. All of you. And I want you to have all of me."

For a moment she stared, her lower lip wobbling, tears hovering in her eyes. When he was sure she'd ask him to leave, she finally took that step. Snaked her arms around his neck and buried her face in his throat. "I love you, Trent. Exactly the way you are. I don't need you to be perfect. I just need you to be here."

Trent released the breath he wasn't aware of holding and crushed her to him. "Jesus."

He was sure he held her so tightly she couldn't breathe, but she didn't complain, and he couldn't let her go. If he did, he'd come apart at the seams. Instead, he buried his face in the fall of hair at her shoulder, let her scent wrap around him and soothe the gaping wound that had opened the morning he'd left her. The warmth of her body made the shaking finally stop.

He turned his head and kissed her neck. "I'm yours, doll. For as long as you'll have me."

She kissed his cheek and leaned back, big brown eyes searching his face. After a moment her gaze dropped to his chest. "You know, the last time we made love, in the kitchen, we didn't…"

He pursed his mouth, his gut churning as that morning rose over him. He'd acted on impulse, something he never did. All he'd known was he was losing her.

"I know. I'm sorry for not being more careful." He shook his head, at a loss as to how to explain. "I wasn't thinking straight. You were ending it, denying me that last day, and I wanted a piece of you to take with me."

She peeked up through her lashes, a soft pink flush rushing into her cheeks. "I'm not. Sorry for it, I mean." One corner of her mouth quirked upward. "That was hot."

He laughed and captured her mouth for a tender kiss, losing himself for a moment in the soft press of her lips against his, then forced himself to pull back. One look at the light and heat in her eyes and he knew. "Marry me."

She froze, her smile melting from her face, gaze searching his. After a moment her brows drew together. "Are you sure?"

"I told you—I don't want to lose you. Ever. What we had? I want that. Every damn day. I want to fall asleep wrapped around you, and I want to wake up next to you and make love to you before I even leave the bed. I want to make you breakfast and come home from work knowing you'll be here waiting for me." He leaned his forehead against hers. "That's bliss."

He'd come home a year and a half ago broken, and in his arms was the woman who'd put him back together. He wasn't ever letting her go.

Tears flooded her eyes again, and she gave him a soft smile. "Yes."

Relief flooded through him. He squeezed her so tight she squeaked, then let out a quiet laugh. Then he released her enough to meet her gaze again. "You should also know I want kids. And I think it's time I got a dog."

Unable to sleep one night, he'd found himself in his closet, staring at all those wooden statues. Then he'd found himself looking up websites on retired service dogs on his phone. The waiting list was long, more than a year, but he wanted one.

The warmth of her palm settled over his heart. "I'm okay with that."

He brushed a kiss across her mouth, then released her and took her hand, sinking to the sofa. Lauren climbed in his lap, straddling his thighs, then wrapped her arms around him and buried her face in his neck. They sat that way for some time, neither one speaking. The rightness of the moment settled inside of him. For the first time since he'd come home, he felt at peace with himself, like he was finally beginning to stitch back together and that maybe, just maybe, morning had finally come, chasing away the darkness within.

Lauren was the first to move. She sat back on his knees and rolled her eyes. "I should probably tell you, Mandy figured out something was up at the party tonight. She noted the tension between us. When I refused to tell her anything, she said if we didn't fix whatever had gone wrong, she'd lock us in a room together."

He could only shake his head. He still wasn't entirely comfortable with his baby sister knowing the details of his sex life. "I suppose that's for the best. I'm going to have to tell her eventually that I'm marrying her best friend."

She laid her head on his shoulder again, and for a few moments a comfortable silence settled between them. He ought to get up, take her to bed. It was late, after all, but he couldn't force himself to move, to relinquish even this small intimacy with her.

"Trent?" Her voice came muffled from his throat.

"Yeah?"

"I'm not sorry, you know." She leaned back again, sitting on his knees. Her gaze caught his for a brief moment, then dropped to his chest, her hand caressing the spot over his heart. "For that month I spent with you. I have no regrets. Even when I thought I'd lost you."

He cupped her cheeks in his palms, letting his thumbs stroke her soft skin. He was a lucky man. "Me either. You made me feel whole again."

Her gaze slid to his, eyes soft and glowing from within. She was happy, and his chest swelled at the sight. Finally. He'd done something to make her happy. He'd try to lasso the moon and the stars in order to keep that look on her face.

Determination lit in her eyes, and Lauren slid off his lap, holding out her hand. "Come on. Time for bed."

He set his hand in hers and let her pull him to his feet, watching the sexy sway of her ass as she led him out of the living room and down the hallway. "To bed or to sleep?"

She shot a smile over her shoulder, but he didn't miss the heat that flared in those gorgeous eyes. "That depends. How tired are you?"

His heart tripped over itself. He hadn't slept in a week. He was exhausted, actually. Bone-dead tired.

Not that he'd tell her that.

He grinned and winked at her. "Not in the least."

Beautiful, sassy, and driven, lawyer Stephanie Mason stopped believing in love a long time ago. So when her military match date ends up being her sexy former college hook-up, Gabe Donovan, she does what any independent, strong woman would: She proposes a no-strings-attached fling. But this former SEAL is determined to convince Steph that, sometimes, love is better the second time around.

See the next page for a preview of
A SEAL's Honor.

CHAPTER ONE

Gabriel Donovan frowned at his reflection in the full-length mirror, then glanced down at his ten-year-old daughter, Charlotte. She stood in front of him, her gaze intent on her task of knotting his tie. "Why the hell am I doing this again?"

Char frowned her disapproval and darted a glance at him. "You owe the swear jar a dollar, Dad. And you're doing this because you need a date. It's time."

With a heavy sigh, he stuffed a hand in his right front pocket, pulled out a dollar bill, and held it out to her. The jar was full already, and the money in there was mostly his. Some example he was setting.

Char stuffed the bill into the pocket of her jeans and resumed knotting his tie. He turned back to his reflection, frowning at the dress shirt and tie she'd insisted he wear. At least he'd won the jeans argument.

He let his shoulders slump. The whole evening set out before him exhausted him, and it hadn't even started. "I am so not cut out for this. I miss your mother."

Life with Julia had been simple. Reliable. She'd been a constant. He'd been cocky enough back in college to think he was good with women, but he hadn't dated in...hell, before Char was born. He was so far out of practice he might as well be a gangly, uncertain teenager all over again.

Char looped one end of the tie over the other and tipped her head back to look up at him. "I miss her, too, Dad, but you promised you wouldn't be sad forever."

While her face remained stoic, her scowl set firm, he didn't miss the worry and sadness that crept into her eyes. Julia's death had been hard on them both but on Char most of all. His baby sister, Molly, was right. A little girl needed her mother. That was also partly why he was going on this date. They both could use a change.

He cupped Char's chin in his palm. She looked like a younger version of Julia. The same auburn hair, a shade darker than her mother's. The same oval face and cute, up-turned nose. All she'd gotten from him were her hazel eyes and unruly curls. Still, every time he saw her, his chest ached. He wasn't ready to start dating again. Marriage and family had suited him fine. "You're too old for your own good, you know that? You shouldn't be taking care of me. You should just be a kid."

Char was smart like her mother, too. She got straight As in school with little effort, constantly had her nose in a book, and since Julia's death, seemed to have made it her mission to take care of him. It's what they'd done since Julia got sick, how they'd gotten by: they took care of each other. Her enthusiasm for his dating again came from a more basic need, though. She wanted him to stop being sad.

At least that's what she'd said last week when he'd finally given in and agreed to his sister's cockamamie scheme. The problem was, he wasn't sure how to stop being sad. How do you stop missing someone when you'd give both arms to have them back?

The heavy emotion in Char's eyes lightened, and she shot him a mischievous smile. That was something else she's gotten from him—her playful nature. "Somebody has to take care of you. We'd eat out every night if I didn't make you cook."

A twinge of guilt of tightened his stomach. She was right, of course. He couldn't cook to save his life. Julia had always taken care of that. Along with a host of other things, like laundry and grocery shopping. Even after his parents' deaths, Molly had taken care of what he'd always considered the "girl stuff." He hated the grocery store. It was too damn crowded and too damn bright. If you asked him, the drive-through was just easier all around.

"I don't know what you have against takeout. Most kids your age could live on the stuff." Gabe turned back to his reflection and poked a finger into his collar, tugging at the tie cinched around his neck. "Is the tie really necessary?"

He hadn't worn one since he'd gotten out of the service four years ago. Spending most of his day at the custom motorcycle and repair shop he co-owned with one of his best friends, Marcus Denali, he had his hands in engine grease the majority of the day. Anything more than a T-shirt would only end up grimy anyway.

Char slipped one end of the tie into the loop she'd made. "Yes. It's nice. Plus, it's blue. That's what they said, right? You have to wear blue so she'll know it's you."

He sighed and stared at his reflection. For the first time since Julia died three years ago, he had a freakin' date, from a service, no less. One of his mechanic's wives owned the exclusive dating service Military Match. Trent Lawson, a fellow SEAL who did most of his custom detailing, had used the place with good results. He and his fiancée, Lauren, were getting married in three months.

"Besides, I like this tie. Mom gave it to you for Christmas before she died. It'll be good luck." Char readjusted his tie and patted his chest, then stood back to eye her handiwork. A self-pleased smile etched across her face. "There. You look perfect."

He shook his head. "I must be out of my mind."

He pinched the bridge of his nose and squeezed his eyes shut for a moment. Three years alone, and he still wasn't ready for this. He was, however, lonely. He missed the simple things, like not having to sleep alone and waking to warm, soft curves. Getting married again, though, he flat out wasn't ready for.

What he hoped for tonight he hadn't a clue. Companionship? To get laid? Someone else to talk to besides Char and Molly and the guys at the shop? Hell. He'd figure out the rest when he got there. At the very least, it would get Molly off his case.

The doorbell sounded through the house, and Char's brows shot up, her eyes widening with excitement.

"That's Aunt Molly!" She darted out of the room, her feet thumping down the hall.

Gabe turned from the full-length floor mirror to the picture on the dresser beside him. He touched the glass, tracing the curve of Julia's forehead with his thumb. She'd been healthy then. Alive and vibrant. Her smile still took his breath away. "Wish me luck, Jules."

He drew a deep breath, trying his damnedest to ignore the nausea swirling in his stomach, and followed Char. Emerging into the front room of the house, he found her in the foyer with Molly. Since Julia's death, Molly had taken to helping him with Char. He was grateful to her on that front, because he was in over his head.

He hadn't a clue how to raise a little girl. If it were up to him, Char would be in the shop with him, learning how to take apart an engine. Julia had always insisted little girls needed a feminine role model. Luckily for him, Char adored her aunt Molly.

Molly glanced up as he entered the living room. A slow smiled curled across her face, amusement gleaming in her eyes. "Wow. Look at you. Hot stuff."

He glared at her as he approached the foyer. "Stop."

Molly's smile drooped. She turned to Char and tousled her hair. "Why you don't go pack your stuff for the weekend. Give me a minute with your dad."

Char shot him a sideways scowl. "Cheer him up, Aunt Molly. He'll ruin his date."

With a shake of her head, Char strode for her bedroom. Once she was out of hearing range, Molly turned worried eyes on him.

Gabe held up a hand, stopping the encouragement he'd heard a dozen times since she'd taken it upon herself to sign him up for this date. "Don't start with the 'this is good for you' crap. I get it. You're both right. It's time. But I don't have to like it."

Molly let out a heavy sigh, then, just as suddenly, flashed an over-bright smile. "At the very least, hope you'll get laid, then."

His heart stalled, and he darted a panicked glance behind him. Char's soft voice echoed up the hallway as she sang some upbeat boy-band tune. Satisfied she hadn't overheard Molly's blatant statement, his heart resumed its beat. Gabe turned back to his sister and frowned.

"Jesus, Moll, keep your voice down." He shouldn't be surprised she'd said it, though. That was Molly in a nutshell—bold as brass and doing as she pleased. He couldn't stop his cheeks from blazing all the same. "I don't need advice on getting laid from my sister."

She had the nerve to grin at him. "Apparently, you do, because you're not doing it."

He glared at her. "Moll…"

She laughed and held up her hands. "All right, all right. At the very least, try to have a good time? Don't scowl, and for crying out loud, don't sit there brooding." She cuffed his shoulder and winked at him. "You had a personality once. Try to dig it up, huh?"

He let out a heavy sigh. She was right. More times than he cared to admit, he'd bitten her head off for worrying about him too much. Hell, the guys at the shop had pointed out the same thing, how snappish he'd become. Marcus had teased him about it the other day, when he'd lost his temper with a supplier over parts that hadn't come in on time. "You need to get laid, man."

Also why he'd found himself with a date tonight. Because Marcus was right. He hadn't had sex with anyone but his left hand since Julia got sick, nearing on four years now. Hell. His freakin' balls were blue. The thought of warm feminine curves against him made his cock twitch in his jeans. If all he got out of this date was that, he'd consider this whole experience successful.

Char came running back to the door, her backpack stuffed full and slung over her shoulder. She hurled herself against him, wrapping her arms tightly around his waist. "Bye, Daddy. I love you."

He bent to kiss the top of her head. "I love you, too, sweetheart. Make sure you mind Aunt Molly, okay?"

She leaned back, hazel eyes wide and anxious and filled with too much worry. "Promise you'll try to have a good time? Mom made me promise that I wouldn't let you sit around and be sad. So you have to promise."

A thick lump formed in his throat. Slayed. Completely, one hundred percent slayed.

He brushed the curls out of her face. "I promise I'll try. Now go."

She hugged him again, then slipped her hand into Molly's.

Molly tossed him a friendly smile. "I'll have her back Sunday morning, as usual."

He hooked his thumbs in his belt loops. "Thanks, Moll. I really appreciate your help, you know."

Warmth bloomed in her eyes, her smile softening. "I know." Then she punched his shoulder and pursed her lips. "Now you have to promise me you're at least going to try to like her."

He couldn't help the soft laugh that left him. Despite being five years younger, she had a definite motherly streak. An annoying one.

He opened the front door and nodded at the porch beyond. "Will you guys get out? I'll never get there with you two hanging around nagging me to death."

Molly rolled her eyes but ushered Char out all the same, calling to him as she made her way to her car, parked at the curb. "I'm going to call you tomorrow morning. You'd better not answer."

He shook his head and closed the door. Alone in the deafening silence, he heaved a sigh. The sickening knots in his gut twisted all over again. The "fun" of this particular dating agency was supposedly in the initial meeting. They set up the time and place, and you simply showed up. All he knew about his date tonight was that she was a blond attorney and she'd be wearing something blue. Hence the damn tie.

According to Karen, the service's owner and his mechanic Mike's wife, the idea was to make the initial meeting seem more like a chance encounter. Add a little mystery. Trent, however, had told him all it really meant was that he'd have a blind date. Trent had loathed that aspect and had offered the information almost as a warning.

Gabe glanced down at his sneakers and stroked a hand down his thigh. At this point, he wasn't above a blind date for his first venture into the land of dating again. He only hoped she wouldn't mind that he was missing the lower part of his left leg.

* * *

Seated on a hard park bench, looking out over the waters of Lake Washington, Stephanie Mason's knee bounced with the nervous anticipation flooding through her. She glanced down at herself, straightening her jacket. A half hour ago, when Lauren, one of her two best friends, suggested she wear this cobalt-blue halter top, it had seemed perfect. A chance to shed the bland suits she wore to the law firm every day, sexy without being too revealing. Now she had her doubts. It seemed too tame.

Were she going to a club, she'd have worn something a little more revealing. She wasn't a stranger to the dating scene. When she had needs, she knew how to flirt, how to dress to lure a man's attention. Lauren, though, the more sensible one of their trio, had pointed out that showing her goods wasn't appropriate for a first date she hoped would lead to more than a one-night stand. The question was, would her date like tame? Or should have insisted on something sexier?

She hitched up the sleeve of her jacket, glanced at her watch for the third time in ten minutes, and heaved a sigh. Her date was late. Okay, so only by five minutes, but in her profession, punctuality was everything. That he was late told her a lot. Namely, that he thought so little of her he couldn't be bothered to show up on time.

So much for the old adage "third time's the charm." This was her third date with Military Match, and it wasn't starting out any better than the others had. The first guy she'd met was so cheap he'd practically squeaked. They'd gone to a matinee show, and he'd paid for dinner with coupons. Freaking coupons. The second guy spent the whole night talking about himself.

Figures that Lauren would go on one date and immediately meet the man she would marry in three months.

Steph glanced down at her top again. Okay, so maybe she should give Lauren more credit. She and Mandy, best friend number two, had dressed Lauren conservative for her date, and looked how that turned out.

She lifted her face to the beautiful sky and stared at the few stars peeking out from between the clouds. She'd known Mandy for two years now, since the day she'd hired the cute brunette to help plan her wedding. When Alec had left her standing at the altar, looking and feeling like an utter fool, Mandy had been the friend she needed. She'd introduced her to her childhood friend Lauren. That night Mandy had insisted on a girls' night at home. They'd had so much fun, they'd immediately made it a weekly thing.

If she'd ever had sisters, those two would've been it.

Which was why she'd taken Lauren's wardrobe suggestions. More than anything, she wanted to meet someone special. Since that day, two years ago now, when Alec had stood her up at the altar, she'd been living a lie, determined never to get hurt like that again. But the truth was, she'd grown tired of the endless flings she'd once convinced herself she delighted in. Deep down she wasn't a single kind of girl, and waking alone every day only served to make her feel exactly that—alone.

Steph turned to scan the area around her again. It being April in the Pacific Northwest, the night was gorgeous. Not quite sixty, with lovely cool breezes and a clear sky, a few stars peeking out from behind the clouds. They usually didn't see days like this until nearly July. Any other time, she'd have put on her Nikes and gone for a run, simply for an excuse to enjoy the break from the ceaseless rain. Apparently, she wasn't alone in that sentiment. A half dozen or so people littered the area.

Her date could be any one of them. Not that she'd recognize him if she saw him. The only information about him the woman from Military Match had given her was that he was "huge," had dark hair, and would be wearing something blue. She was told to meet him by the beach, here at Chism Park.

Restless with the need to move, she surged to her feet and turned in a slow circle. Halfway around, a sight stopped her cold. Some twenty feet or so down the sidewalk, a huge hulk of a man stood doing exactly what she was. Hands stuffed in his pockets, he looked around, as if he were waiting for someone.

The width of his strong shoulders and the dark hair licking at the collar of his black leather jacket sent her stomach into overdrive. The ache of familiarity flooded her veins, setting her heart to trying to escape her chest.

Gabe.

God, he looked exactly the same as the last time she'd seen him. Had it really been eleven years? He stood six foot six inches of intimidating, delicious man. His hair curled over his forehead, the ends whipping in the slight breeze. Her hands itched with remembrance. How many times had she brushed those curls out of his eyes?

Back in college, undergrad days, those big hands and that muscular body had given her so much pleasure. Of all her lovers over the years, he was the one she couldn't forget. He'd been one of the few to truly rock her world. The energy they'd worked up in each other could easily have powered a small city.

He'd also been one of the few to manage the feat of capturing her heart. Her one and only foray into how to do everything wrong. She'd fallen in love with her best friend. Eleven years ago she and Gabe had fallen into a friends-with-benefits relationship. They'd hung out, discussing classes and dick professors while sharing cartons of Chinese as often as they'd fucked.

Of course, the bigger question was…was he tonight's date?

The thought made her stomach flip-flop. What she wanted was to turn around and run. Of all the men she could have ended up with tonight, it had to be him. She was here, though, and curiosity had her by the heart. She'd thought of him often over the years.

Besides, Steph Mason didn't run from anything.

She drew her shoulders back, plastered on her best "no care in the world" smile, and sauntered in his direction. "Gabriel Donovan."

His head snapped in her direction, and familiar hazel eyes settled on her. Oh, she didn't have to see them to know their color. She'd know those eyes anywhere, because she'd spent years trying not to stare at them. Beautiful and intense, they were a mix of chocolate brown and a deep, mossy green. They widened as recognition dawned over him. "Stephanie Mason. I'll be damned."

As she came to a stop in front of him, she had to tip her head back to look into his face. He stood a good head above her, and she shivered with the power of that broad body.

"The last time I saw you, you were crawling out of my bed." She attempted to keep the conversation light, but the truth was, the last night they were together, Gabe had gotten a phone call that changed his entire world. His parents had died a tragic, senseless death, literally at the wrong place at the wrong time. A robbery attempt gone wrong had left him suddenly in charge of his teenaged sister. Gabe had dropped out of school a week later and moved home to Oregon to take care of Molly.

"Been a long time, Steph." He grinned, revealing a dazzling smile that eleven years ago would have taken her breath away. Now it sent more memories flooding through her mind. That playful smile had drawn her in the first time he'd flashed it at her.

"That it has. Last I heard from you, you'd joined the navy. They were stationing you in California." They'd kept in touch for a while after he went home but had slowly lost track of each other over the years.

He gave an absentminded nod. "Camp Coronado. It's where I did my BUD/S training."

Buds training... Where had she heard that term before? Wait a minute... "You were a SEAL?"

He darted a glance at her. "Team three. Moved back here about four years ago."

She nudged him with an elbow. "Seriously impressive."

He didn't say anything, but seemed to draw within himself. His gaze slid off to his right, and awkward tension moved over him. She searched her thoughts for something, anything, to pull him out of what seemed to be heavy thoughts, when her gaze settled on his tie. The sapphire blue stood out against the stark white of his shirt. Damn. That tie meant Gabe was her date.

Well, the only thing to do now was face it head-on. The way she did everything.

She drew a deep breath for courage and tugged on his tie. "Blue."

His gaze snapped back to her, dropped to his tie, then returned to her again. One corner of his mouth hitched. He nodded in her direction, no doubt indicating the similar color of her shirt. Amusement and recognition glinted in his eyes. "Also blue."

"That makes you the date I've been waiting for." She couldn't be sure if she wanted to hug the stuffing out of him or puke on his shoes. Despite everything, it was good to see him. She had to admit, if only to herself, she'd missed him.

He shook his head, reached up to rub the back of his neck, and glanced around him. "Sorry I'm late. Forgot what part of the park we were supposed to meet at. I swore I wrote it down, but I couldn't find the damn note."

She lifted a brow. "Nervous?"

For that one small thing, she was eternally grateful. At least she wasn't the only one coming out of her skin. She'd thought about this moment a lot over the years. Where he was, what his life was like, what she'd do if she ever saw him again. She hadn't anticipated the power of being in his presence again, though. In the courtroom, she could hold her own. Here with him? Her knees were shaking.

He let out an uncomfortable laugh. "Does it show?"

"Nope. You're as solid as ever. Don't feel bad. This date has my stomach tied into knots on top of knots." Unable to contain her excitement any longer, she punched him lightly in the shoulder. "How the hell are you?"

"I'm good." Gabe laughed, his gaze sweeping the length of her. "You haven't changed a bit. Still as sexy as ever. The hair's changed, though. You had a pixie cut last I saw you. Long looks good on you."

The husky timbre of his voice made her nipples tighten. Whether consciously or otherwise, he reached out and pushed her hair back off her shoulder, his fingers brushing the skin of her neck. A full-out shiver swept the length of her spine. God, she was doomed. One touch from him sent fire burning through her blood.

"You're still the same. Same curls, same crooked smile." He had lines around his eyes now, but she liked them. They lent his appearance a maturity that looked good on him. As if it were possible for Gabe Donovan to get any sexier.

He dropped his hand, his mouth forming a thin line. Something somber moved over him and the playful air between them shifted. "I've changed. Parts of me, at least."

She frowned, trying to comprehend the sudden tension moving over him. That was the second time in five minutes he'd gotten that look on his face. It was subtle but undeniable.

He stared at her for a beat, then slid his hand down his left thigh, inching the pant leg of his jeans up enough to reveal his ankle. Or at least, what should have been an ankle. Instead, there was a metal rod attached to some sort of plastic device. It took all of two seconds to realize what he was showing her. Gabe had lost his leg.

"Oh my God." Her breath caught in a suddenly full throat as the aching realization punched her in the chest. Her eyes misted, a million horror-filled visions floating through her mind. Namely, how he'd lost it. Was it a roadside bomb? Or a suicide bomber? The thought of him in any one of the possibilities made breathing impossible. God, now she really wanted to hug the stuffing out of him.

She stroked her hand down his thigh, following the length of his leg. The muscle beneath tensed, but he didn't pull away or ask her to stop. Her hand smoothed over solid muscle, then over the bone of his knee. So he had that much at least.

When she looked up at him again, he stood with his shoulders drawn back, mouth a thin, tight line. Those hazel eyes searched hers. Anxious. Waiting.

Her minded shifted gears, and her face heated. God, what her reaction must seem to him. She drew back her trembling hand and straightened. *Pull it together.*

"I'm sorry. You surprised me. I'm imagining the pain, how it must have happened…" Despite her best effort, her voice wobbled, and she let the rest of the sentence float off on the breeze. She must look like a blubbering idiot. She was a divorce attorney for one of the best firms in the city. Not much surprised her or frightened her anymore. But the thought of him wounded had her heart in a vise.

He stared at her for a beat, eyes reaching and searching. Whatever he looked for, he seemed to find, for he cupped her chin in his palm and stroked her skin with his thumb. The tension in his body dissipated. "I'm alive and otherwise whole. It's just a foot."

She rolled her eyes. "Leave it to you to make a joke of it. Clearly you haven't changed."

He dropped his hand and held out his elbow instead. "Walk with me?"

She nodded, took his proffered elbow, and they started off, following the trail leading around the lake. All things considered, he walked well, with the same smooth, lanky gait he'd had years ago. If he hadn't shown her his prosthesis, she wouldn't have suspected.

"I lost the leg in Iraq, a little over four years ago. My third stint over there. I was on a truck at the end of a convoy that was hit by a bazooka rocket. We were acting as support for the local militia when we were ambushed."

"Did it hurt?" Another stupid question, but she was having a hard time with this one. She couldn't stop picturing him on that truck—the rocket exploding through the men, him being hurled from the vehicle. Her chest constricted and tears filled her eyes all over again.

"Oddly enough, not at first. It's how I knew something was wrong. I couldn't feel my leg. Hurt like a bitch when I came to in the hospital, though. It was a lot of physical therapy and learning how to walk again. Now…" He shrugged. "I'm used to it. It's just another part of me, I guess."

"You were nervous, though, telling me." She glanced up at him, offering him an apologetic frown. "I'm sorry about my reaction. It wasn't the leg. It was just…a shock, I guess. I'm still picturing you running circles around me and teasing me for being so slow."

They'd originally met because they'd run the same loop around the University of Washington campus. She'd passed him every day. One evening he'd jogged up beside her and started a conversation that launched a thousand others.

"I can still run circles around you." He playfully bumped her shoulder; then somberness settled over him again. "You're not the first person I've told, but it's never easy to do. I never know how people will react. Some people can't handle it."

She squeezed his biceps. "I am sorry. I should have stopped to think about how that would seem to you."

"Forget about it. The look on your face told me what you were thinking right then."

She let out a quiet laugh. "I've never had a great poker face."

He glided to a stop and turned to her. The quiet, all-too-familiar intensity of his gaze made her shiver in spite of herself. "Apparently we're stuck together for the evening. How 'bout some dinner?"

She shouldn't. Since her breakup with Alec, she hadn't had anything resembling a normal relationship. When she'd agreed to this date, she'd wanted a middle road, a first step, and history told her that nothing with Gabe would ever be uncomplicated. He was here, though, and she couldn't deny that for eleven years she'd been dying to catch up with him.

She smiled. "Sounds great."

Acknowledgments

I have a few people I'd like to send out my gratitude to. First off, to author Vonnie Davis for being generous enough to share her knowledge of the SEALs with a (slightly) overwhelmed author. I can never thank you enough, V!

To a few of the ladies on my street team, Jo's Jewels, particularly Terri Rochenski, Nicole Lieren, Kathryn Knight, Bette, Shawnee, Jennifer Wilck, and Angela, for letting me pick their brains during revisions.

And to Pat, Shelly, Debbie, Dixie, Rosemary, Tina, and Judith, also on my street team. For your love and support and for picking me up on those days when my ego had taken a beating. So honored to know you ladies!

I can't write this without sending a special thanks to my editor, Jessie, for doing what she does best and for taking my book and helping me to make it shine. You make me actually enjoy editing. Who knew?! LOL.

Last, but not least, I have to stop and thank my agent, Dawn Dowdle, for her continuous support and positive energy.

About the Author

JM Stewart is a coffee and chocolate addict who lives in the Pacific Northwest with her husband, two sons, and two very spoiled dogs. She's a hopeless romantic who believes everybody should have their happily ever after and has been devouring romance novels for as long as she can remember. Writing them has become her obsession.

Learn more at:
AuthorJMStewart.com
Facebook.com/AuthorJMStewart
Twitter: @JMStewartWriter

9 781538 728840